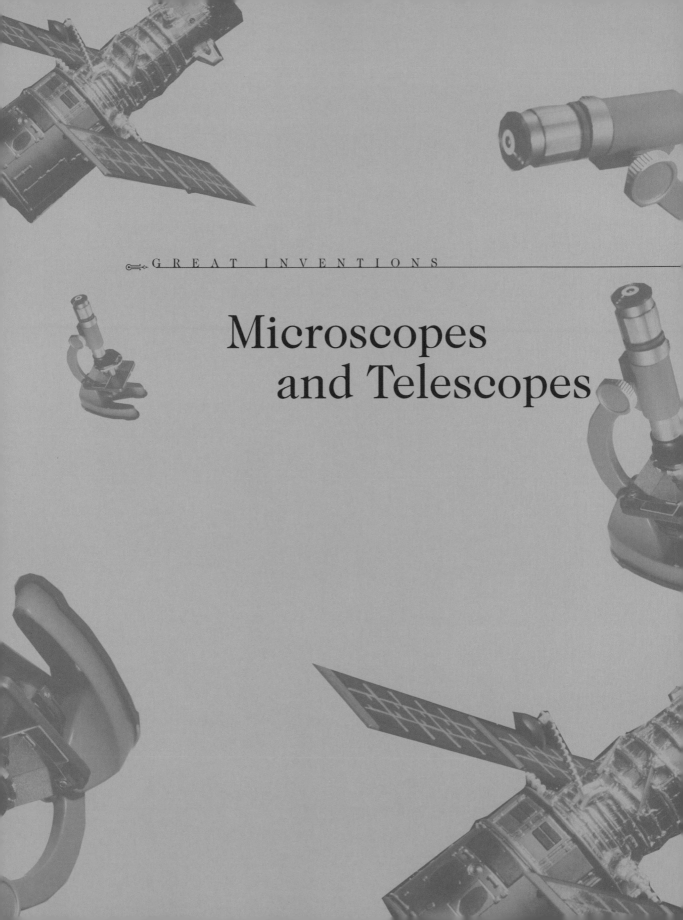

# Microscopes and Telescopes

GREAT INVENTIONS

# Microscopes and Telescopes

REBECCA STEFOFF

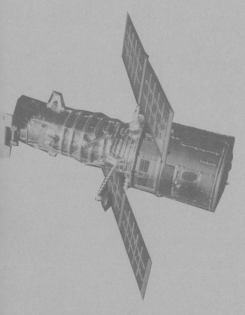

**mc** **Marshall Cavendish**
Benchmark
New York

Marshall Cavendish Benchmark
99 White Plains Road
Tarrytown, NY 10591-9001
www.marshallcavendish.us

Library of Congress Cataloging-in-Publication Data

Stefoff, Rebecca, 1951–
Microscopes and telescopes / by Rebecca Stefoff.
p. cm.—(Great inventions)
Summary: "An exploration of the origins, history, development, and
societal impact of the microscope and the telescope"—Provided by publisher.
Includes bibliographical references and index.
ISBN-13: 978-0-7614-2230-3
ISBN-10: 0-7614-2230-7
1. Microscopes—Juvenile literature. 2. Telescopes—Juvenile literature.
I. Title. II. Series: Great inventions (Marshall Cavendish Benchmark)

QH211.S77 2006
502.8'2—dc22

2005037558

Series design by Sonia Chaghatzbanian

Photo research by Candlepants Incorporated

Cover photo: SW Productions/GettyImages

The photographs in this book are used by permission and through the courtesy of: *The Image Works:* SSPL, 2, 73; photri/Topham, 50; NASA/SSPL, 65; 68; Ann Ronan Picture Library/HIP, 83, 87. *Photo Researchers Inc.:* John R. Foster, 8; Science Picture Library, 25, 82; Bryan & Cherry Alexander, 33; Larry Landolfi, 46; David Nunik, 58; David Parker, 60, 94, 96; Jean-Loup Charmet, 80. *Corbis:* Bettmann, 15, 39, 75; Archivo Iconographico, S.A., 28, 37; Christel Gerstenberg, 41; Roger Ressmeyer, 42, 52; Firefly Productions, 44, 101; Joseph Sohm/Visions of America, 55; Denis Scott, 62; Thom Lang, 70; Visuals Unlimited, 79; Mathias Kulka, 95; ER Productions, 104-105. *Art Resource, New York:* Scala, 18, 22; HIP, 26, 77. *Getty Images:* Josef Fankhauser, 31; Dorothy Riess MD, 99. *SuperStock:* age fotostock, 102.

Printed in China
1 3 5 6 4 2

# CONTENTS

# Microscopes and Telescopes

AN AMATEUR ASTRONOMER STUDIES THE SKY. SOME BACKYARD STARGAZERS NOW USE TELE-SCOPES AS GOOD AS, OR BETTER THAN, THE PROFESSIONAL INSTRUMENTS OF A CENTURY AGO.

# It Started with Spectacles

The Italian astronomer and mathematician Galileo Galilei was more than a brilliant scientist. He was also a practical craftsman, and if he happened to hear or read that someone had created a new scientific instrument, he would make one for himself. Around 1609 Galileo made his own versions of two new pieces of equipment. They were the microscope and the telescope, destined to transform people's understanding of the world around them. Although Galileo invented neither instrument, he improved on both of them. Galileo also used the telescope to make remarkable discoveries that revolutionized astronomy—and could have gotten him killed.

The microscope and the telescope introduced new ways of observing the universe, both the immediate world and worlds far distant. Microscopes enlarged small objects close at hand, letting people see things that are too tiny to be viewed with the unaided eye. They revealed intricate, invisible worlds: tiny creatures swimming in drops of water, the crystalline structure of common minerals such as salt, the cells that make up living things, and eventually the individual atoms that are the building blocks of all matter. Telescopes, in contrast, made distant things larger and easier to see. Through the telescope, objects that people hadn't even known existed suddenly came into view.

# Basic Optics: Refraction

The magnifying glass and the optical microscope consist of lenses, as does the refracting telescope, the first type of telescope invented. All of these instruments make use of the way lenses refract, or bend, light. The angle of the refraction depends on the shape of the lens.

The two basic lens shapes are convex and concave. Convex lens surfaces curve outward, so that the lens is thicker in the center than at the edges. Concave surfaces curve inward, so that the lens is thicker at the edges than in the center. One or both surfaces may be curved. Different kinds of lenses can be fused together to form compound lenses (a compound lens is not the same as a compound instrument, which is an instrument with more than one lens).

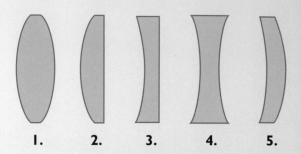

1.  2.  3.  4.  5.

When light passes through a convex surface, the light rays are refracted so that they meet, or focus, at a spot on the other side of the lens. This focusing of light rays is called convergence. The place where the rays meet is the focal point; the distance from the center of the lens to the focal point is the lens's focal length. Light rays that pass through a concave surface, however, are refracted outward in a cone-shaped pattern, a spreading of the rays that is known as divergence.

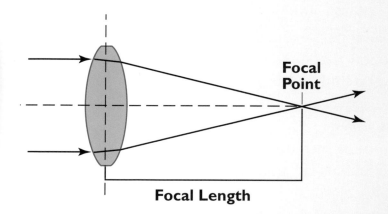

Focal Point

Focal Length

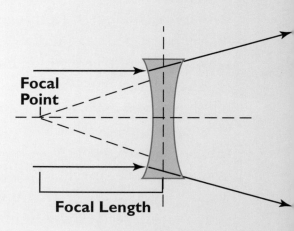

Focal Point

Focal Length

The lens of a human eye converges light at a focal point on the retina, the inner wall of the eye. But if the shape of the lens is a little bit off, the focal point will be a slightly behind or in front of the retina, causing either presbyopia (far-sightedness, which can be corrected with convex eyeglass lenses) or myopia (near-sightedness, corrected with concave lenses). Like the lens of a human eye, a magnifying glass is a biconvex lens. It makes things look bigger by bending light rays to create an image of the object being examined.

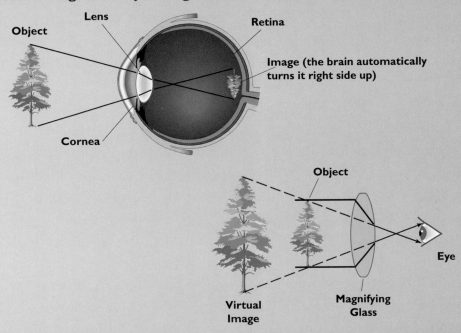

Some early microscopes had just one lens. These simple microscopes, as single-lens instruments are called, were essentially magnifying glasses held in frames or tubes. Other early microscopes, however, had several lenses, as did the first telescopes. In instruments such as these, a lens or set of lenses called the objective focuses the incoming light. The resulting image is viewed through a second lens or set of lenses known as the eyepiece. The use of multiple lenses increases the magnifying power of the instrument.

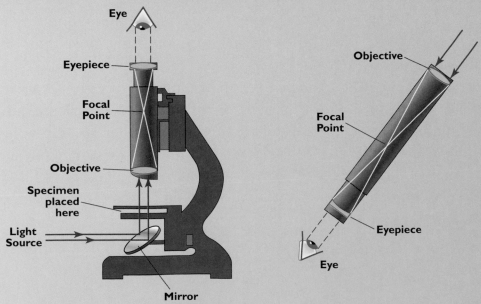

The microscope and the telescope extended human vision in opposite directions—one probing inward, the other outward—but the two instruments grew from the same roots. Both are based in optics, the science of light and its properties. And although the identities of those who invented these important devices are somewhat mysterious, both instruments originated in the shops of the spectacle-makers who flourished in the Netherlands in the late sixteenth and early seventeenth centuries.

Spectacles, or eyeglasses, themselves were a wondrous invention. For people whose abilities were limited by weak or defective vision, or those whose sight was failing with old age, they seemed miraculous. Spectacles corrected and strengthened vision by harnessing the basic optical properties of lenses, which are transparent disks with one or both sides curved. If both sides of a clear disk are flat, it is not a lens. It is simply a small piece of glass like a miniature windowpane. Light passes through it unchanged. But curved surfaces on a transparent material refract, or bend, the light that passes through the material. The direction and degree of refraction depend on the shape of the curve.

Since ancient times people have known that lenses can magnify objects, making them appear larger. Disks of a transparent, naturally occurring form of quartz called rock crystal have been found in archaeological sites in Egypt, Turkey, Greece, England, Sweden, and elsewhere. Ground or polished into convex shapes, these became the first magnifying lenses. Although some researchers point out that there is no proof that these crystals were anything more than decorative ornaments, other historians of optics think that the ancients may have used them the way some people use magnifying glasses today—as aids in seeing or in performing detailed, small-scale work such as jewelry-making. An early reference to the magnifier as a reading aid comes from the Roman playwright and philosopher Seneca, who lived in the first century C.E. Seneca wrote that a clear glass bowl filled with water, when placed on a page, made written characters larger and easier to read. Such a bowl forms a convex lens. The surface of the water is the flat side of the lens, and the bottom of the bowl is the curved side. The bowl would magnify letters just as a magnifying glass does. Neither a bowl of water or any of the ancient rock-crystal lenses, however, would have been suitable for a telescope. No reliable evidence suggests that either a telescope or a true microscope existed until after the grinding of lenses for spectacles had become a profession.

The origin of spectacles is a mystery in itself. Islamic writings from the eleventh century show that scholars in the Muslim world understood the basic principles of refraction and magnification. These writings were known to two English philosophers of the early thirteenth century, Robert Grosseteste and Roger Bacon, both of whom wrote about light and optics. Philosopher and scientist Bacon said that a section of a solid glass sphere—in other words, a lens with one flat side and one convex side—would magnify things viewed through it. "For this reason," he wrote, "such an instrument is useful to old persons and to those with weak sight, for they can see any letter, however small, if magnified enough." Like Seneca with his bowl of water, Bacon recognized the magnifying power of the lens as an aid to reading. By the time he wrote those words, in fact, people were probably already using crystal or glass magnifiers as reading aids.

Around the end of the thirteenth century, someone fastened two lenses together side by side and created the first pair of eyeglasses. Despite a wealth of hints, rumors, and claims, the inventor will probably never be known for certain. Spectacles may have originated in Italy, most likely in one of the northern cities such as Pisa or Florence. One of the earliest references to their possible origins is a quote from a 1305 sermon by Fra Giordano da Rivalto of Pisa, who wrote, "It is not yet twenty years that the art of making glasses was invented; this enables good sight and is one of the best as well as the most useful of arts that the world possesses."

Within a few decades, spectacles were known throughout Europe. Artists in the mid-fourteenth century started featuring eyeglasses in their paintings, often placing them on the faces of people who lived centuries before glasses were invented, such as the ancient Roman poet Virgil and even characters from biblical stories. Nobles, scholars, merchants, and craftspeople who could afford the costly curiosities prized them. Documents such as wills, inventories of possessions, and court papers dating from the fourteenth century show that eyeglasses were treasured belongings, passed carefully from one owner to the next.

These early spectacles were different from modern glasses. They were simply lenses in a frame that the user held in place before the eyes by hand or with a stick attached to one side, or tied in place with a string around the head; the earpieces we use today were not added until several centuries later. All of the early eyeglasses had biconvex lenses that bulged outward on both surfaces. (This shape, resembling a lentil, was the source of the word *lens*, which is Latin for "lentil.") These lenses could correct far-sightedness, which is the inability to focus on near objects. Correcting near-sightedness, the inability to focus on distant objects, called for concave lenses, which are more difficult to grind than convex ones. Not until the mid-fifteenth or early sixteenth century did lens grinders begin producing concave lenses.

By the sixteenth century the Netherlands had become a center of spectacle making, with numerous lens grinders working in each of its major cities. The stage was set for someone to combine spectacle lenses in new ways, creating the first microscope and the first telescope, each of which was simply a convex lens and a concave lens, placed the right distance apart inside a tube that made the image clearer by shutting out the surrounding light.

Who was the first to do so? Historians may never know. The invention of both the microscope and the telescope is shrouded in confusion and counterclaims. The microscope seems to have appeared first, around 1590. Hans (or Johannes) and Zacharias Janssen, a father-and-son team of Dutch spectacle makers, were once called the inventors of the microscope, but the first written references to them as the inventors of the instrument date from some years later, in the seventeenth century, and modern historians have rejected them as the origin of the microscope. The Janssens are known to have produced some microscopes in the early seventeenth century, but by that time the instrument had become widely known, and a number of other lens grinders had been making microscopes for years.

The Janssens also claimed to have invented the telescope, but telescope historians do not take their claim seriously. The true origins of the telescope, however, are as murky as those of the microscope. Hans Lippershey or Lipperhey, a spectacle maker in the Dutch town of Middelburg,

AN ARTIST'S IMPRESSION OF HANS LIPPERSHEY INVENTING THE TELESCOPE. IN REALITY LIPPERSHEY WAS MOST LIKELY JUST ONE OF SEVERAL LENS GRINDERS AND SPECTACLE MAKERS WHO CREATED THE FIRST TELESCOPES AROUND 1608.

generally receives credit for the invention. All that historians know for certain, however, is that Lippershey was the first to try to make money from the telescope. On September 30, 1608, Lippershey presented himself to Maurice of Nassau, ruler of the Netherlands, offering to give the ruler "a certain device, by means of which all things at a very great distance can be seen as if they were nearby." That device was a telescope that Lippershey said he had invented. In *Stargazer: The Life and Times of the Telescope* (2004), astronomer Fred Watson explains that "the lenses Lipperhey had at his disposal would probably have restricted the magnification of his telescope to about three times." Not much magnification, by modern standards—about the same as a pair of the inexpensive small binoculars known as opera glasses. Still, it would astound someone who had never had the experience of peering into an eyepiece and seeing a distant building suddenly appear close. Maurice was impressed.

At the time, the Netherlands and Spain had been at war for years but were in the middle of peace negotiations. A Spanish diplomat named Ambrogio Spinola happened to be present when Maurice examined Lippershey's device. Within days, Spinola had told his own government about the new instrument. Meanwhile, Maurice passed the instrument on to the States General, the Dutch government. The ruler mentioned that the device would be handy for keeping an eye on "the tricks of the enemy," although he failed to mention that the enemy— or at least its representative, Spinola—had already seen the device and even looked through it. Around the same time, Lippershey asked the States General to grant him either a patent, which would mean that for thirty years he would be the only one who could legally make telescopes in the Netherlands, or a yearly pension. The government agreed to consider his request. Meanwhile, it ordered Lippershey to make six more similar devices. These would be binoculars, rather than telescopes, because they were to have a set of lenses for each eye.

Almost at once, however, controversy erupted. First, a maker of scientific instruments from the town of Alkmaar stepped forward to claim that *he* had invented the telescope. Then the States General received a letter on behalf of a third inventor, claiming that still other makers of spectacles and instruments also knew how to make far-seeing devices. Even before this cluster of competing claims sprang up in the Netherlands, two English thinkers—Thomas Digges around 1570 and William Bourne in 1578—had written descriptions of optical instruments that some historians have interpreted as telescopes. Neither Digges nor Bourne claimed to have built a telescope, however, and some modern experts think that their descriptions were simply speculations about imaginary devices. Then, in 1589, Giovanbaptista della Porta of Italy wrote that he had found a way to use convex and concave lenses together to improve both distant and close vision. Although a few researchers have interpreted this as an early account of a telescope, others think that della Porta actually wrote the first known description of bifocals, or eyeglasses with combination lenses, although it is not known whether he actually made a pair of such glasses.

So who did invent the telescope? Like the microscope, it probably had multiple inventors. Telescopes could have come into existence in various workshops, around the same time, created independently by people who were working with lenses, either manufacturing them or studying their optical properties. The details of who invented what are less important than the effects of the two new instruments on human knowledge. By extending vision beyond the limits of the eye, both the microscope and the telescope would reveal whole realms of existence that were previously unknown. The telescope's impact would be felt first.

Confronted with a cluster of claims by rival telescope makers, the Dutch government decided that the instrument was too widely known and copied to belong to a single inventor. The States General therefore refused to grant either a patent or a pension to Lippershey or any other claimant. This meant that anyone who heard about the marvel-

MATHEMATICIAN AND EXPERIMENTER GALILEO GALILEI (1597-1681) USED HIS MASTERY OF THE LAWS OF OPTICS—THE BEHAVIOR OF LIGHT—TO IMPROVE BOTH THE MICROSCOPE AND THE TELESCOPE. WITH TELESCOPES HE HAD BUILT, HE MADE STARTLING DISCOVERIES ABOUT THE HEAVENLY BODIES.

lous new device was free to copy it—and word of the innovation traveled surprisingly fast. In early-seventeenth-century Europe, scholars, educated people, and scientific experimenters exchanged letters that were often passed from hand to hand among many readers. Diplomats and other travelers also provided information about events in other countries. One such diplomat was Guido Bentivoglio, an Italian representative of the pope who was present when the Spanish diplomat Spinola told his superiors about the telescope. Bentivoglio not only wrote to friends in Italy about the new device but by April 1609 had managed to get hold of one and send it to Rome. News of the instrument spread in other directions, too. About six weeks after Lippershey gave his telescope to Maurice, a Parisian wrote in his diary about hearing of the new invention. In April 1609 the same diarist saw telescopes for sale in the shop of a French spectacle maker.

Up to this point, people regarded the telescope as a tool for getting better views of distant objects on Earth. Used this way, the telescope was often called a spyglass; today it is usually termed a terrestrial telescope. Soon, though, an English scientist named Thomas Harriot turned the telescope in a different direction and found a new use for it. After hearing about the new Dutch instruments, Harriot either bought or built one of his own and became the first person to record astronomical observations made through a telescope. On July 26, 1609, Harriot drew the earliest known sketch of the Moon's surface as seen through a telescope, or "cylinder," as he called it. Harriot's pupil William Lower also made telescopic observations of the full Moon, which he said looked "like a tart that my cooke made me last weeke; here a vaine of bright stuffe, and there of darke, and so confusedlie all over. I must confesse I can see none of this without my cylinder."

By May or June 1609 word of the new instrument had reached Galileo Galilei, a mathematics professor at the University of Padua, near Venice, Italy. At once Galileo was, as he later wrote, "seized with a desire for the beautiful thing." He decided to manufacture one, and soon he found a combination of lenses that duplicated Lippershey's spyglass, or *perspicillum,* as Galileo called it. Using ready-made spectacle lenses, Galileo fixed a plano-convex lens in one end of a lead tube and a plano-concave lens at the other end to serve as an eyepiece. In *Seeing and Believing* (2000), a history of the telescope, Richard Panek points out that Galileo did more than simply make a scientific instrument. He reached an important understanding of how the instrument works. Galileo, says Panek, "used his knowledge of optics to figure out the mathematical relationship at the heart of the device's power to magnify: the ratio of the focal lengths." Galileo discovered if he fitted a spyglass with a lens at the far end that brought images to a focus twelve inches away, and a second lens at the near end that brought images to a focus four inches away, the spyglass magnified images three times—twelve divided by four. "Once he'd figured out this formula," says Panek, "it would have been relatively simple for someone with Galileo's technical expertise to grind new lenses to exploit this mathematical relationship to best advantage."

Galileo was indeed a capable lens grinder and instrument maker. Soon after he experimented with the telescope, he constructed a magnifying device for seeing small things close-up, using a convex and a concave lens. Galileo modeled this magnifier on the microscopes that the Dutch had been making for two decades but improved it with his new understanding of focal lengths. He called the device an *occhialino* and later made several more, presenting them as gifts to the king of Poland and to the Academy of the Lynx, a scientific and philosophical society based in Rome. Through his *occhialino,* Galileo observed such things as the hooked feet that allow a fly to walk on a ceiling. Yet the *occhialino* was not destined to hold Galileo's interest the way his *perspicillum* did. The wonders of the microscopic world would be left for others to discover—Galileo would look to the skies.

From the start, Galileo was aware of the practical possibilities of the telescope for terrestrial use. When he presented a *perspicillum* to the leaders of Venice, he sent along a letter outlining the military advantages of seeing the ships and troops of an enemy "before he detects us" and of being able to look inside enemy fortresses from far away. But Galileo also used his telescope to see the night sky in a new way. One of the first things he examined was the surface of the Moon. As he later wrote, "the Moon is by no means endowed with a smooth and polished surface, but is rough and uneven and, just as the face of Earth itself, crowded everywhere with vast prominences, deep chasms, and convolutions." The phrase "just as the face of Earth itself" sums up what historians of science now consider a vital aspect of Galileo's astronomical studies. For centuries, people had regarded the heavens as a realm completely apart from Earth, made of different, finer material, perfect and unchanging. By seeing that the surface of the Moon had geographic features similar to those of Earth, Galileo and other early telescope users showed that the heavens are not a separate realm but are part of the same universe as the Earth, with similar materials and physical properties.

By November 1609 Galileo had created a telescope that magnified twenty times (later he would make a thirty-power instrument). He began a program of systematic astronomical observations that, in revealing truths about the solar system, would put the astronomer on a collision course with the Roman Catholic Church. Although Galileo's stargazing took place privately, in the garden behind his Padua apartment, it brought him into a dangerous public debate about cosmology, which is the structure of the cosmos, or universe.

Cosmological questions were not new. Since ancient times people had developed theories about the shape of the world and the universe. Their ideas were based on what they observed: the rising and setting of the Sun and Moon, the movement of the stars across the night sky over the course of a year, the motions of the planets as they wandered among the stars. For thousands of years the most widely held cosmological view was that the Earth stood still at the center of the universe, with the Sun, Moon, planets, and stars all revolving around it. A few thinkers challenged that view—in the third century B.C.E., for example,

ONE OF GALILEO'S TELESCOPES. HIS BEST INSTRUMENT MAGNIFIED OBJECTS BY ABOUT THIRTY TIMES.

the Greek philosopher Aristarchus of Samos claimed that the Earth moved, rotating on its axis and revolving around the Sun. Aristarchus was right, but the idea of an Earth-centered universe was too well-established to be easily overthown. Saying that the Earth moved seemed to violate common sense—it didn't *feel* as though it were moving. So Aristarchus's insight was forgotten, and people continued to think of Earth as the center of the universe. Enshrined in the writings of two of the ancient world's most famous thinkers—the philosopher and scientist Aristotle and the geographer and astronomer Ptolemy—the geocentric or Earth-centered universe became the accepted cosmology of Renaissance Europe.

A major challenge to the traditional geocentric or Ptolemaic view appeared in the 1543 book *De revolutionibus orbium coelestium* (On the Revolution of the Heavenly Spheres), by Nicolaus Copernicus, a Polish clergyman and astonomer. Copernicus argued that the Sun was at the center of the universe and that the Earth was one of the planets that revolved around it. The appearance of a rising and setting Sun was due to the daily rotation of the Earth on its axis. One common objection to this theory was that if the Earth were truly spinning, as Copernicus claimed, everything would be flung off its surface. Copernicus could not explain why this did not happen, because gravity was not yet understood, but he insisted that the universe was heliocentric, or Sun-centered, and that the Earth moved through it.

For decades after Copernicus's theory was published, astronomers, philosophers, and other scientists wrestled with it. Religion was at issue, as well as science. The Christian faith, and especially the leaders of the Roman Catholic Church, staunchly opposed Copernicanism because it seemed to conflict with passages in the Bible. In the Church's view, Earth, the scene of biblical history and of Christ's birth and death, must be stationary at the center of the universe. The heavenly bodies must revolve around Earth in circular orbits because the circle was a perfect, ideal form. For this reason, although Copernicus had claimed that the heliocentric universe was a physical fact and not simply a mathematical theory, other thinkers accepted Copernicus's detailed observations of planetary movements and star positions without accepting his heliocentrism. The last great astronomer of the pre-telescope era, Tycho Brahe, adopted this approach. Brahe established an observatory in Denmark and built the finest instruments then available for sighting the stars and planets and measuring their positions in the sky, but he died in 1601, still believing in the geocentric universe, before the telescope was known.

During his last year, Brahe employed as his assistant a mathematics teacher named Johannes Kepler. Unlike his employer, Kepler was convinced of the truth of Copernicus's heliocentric model of the universe. Using the wealth of observations that Brahe had compiled over the years, Kepler set out to prove that Copernicus was right. By the time Kepler started pursuing this goal, several other late-sixteenth-century European thinkers had published radical ideas about the cosmos. Giordano Bruno of Italy claimed that the universe was infinitely large, not bounded by a shell of stars as people had traditionally believed. Bruno also asserted that the Sun was a star and that the other stars were suns, and that "numberless Earths" might revolve around those suns. These other worlds could be inhabited by beings equal to earthly creatures, he claimed, or even superior to them. Although Bruno was not the only thinker who wrote about such possibilities, he was unlucky enough to anger officials of the Roman Catholic Church, which regarded his ideas on many topics as heresy, or violations of church doctrine. In 1600 the church burned Bruno alive at the stake in Rome, in part for his views on cosmology. Against this ominous background Galileo began his astronomical observations nine years later.

In early 1610, not long after Galileo started studying the sky through his telescope, he published a book titled *Sidereus nuncius* (Starry messenger). It described a series of startling discoveries about the heavens: mountains and craters on the Moon; dark spots on the

ITALIAN PHILOSOPHER GIORDANO BRUNO (1548-1600) WAS BURNED ALIVE AT THE STAKE IN ROME. THE CHURCH EXECUTED HIM IN PART BECAUSE OF HIS IDEAS ABOUT THE STRUCTURE OF THE UNIVERSE—IDEAS THAT GALILEO AND OTHERS SOON ECHOED.

surface of the Sun; hundreds of new stars, previously unseen, in familiar constellations such as Orion; clouds of individual stars where the unaided eye saw only the pale glowing band called the Milky Way. Galileo's most sensational discovery, though, was that the planet Jupiter had four satellites that orbited it just as the Moon orbits the Earth. This was the first time anyone had considered that another planet might have moons. With an eye to his own career, Galileo called the satellites "Medicean stars" in honor of Cosimo II de Medici, grand duke of Tuscany, who promptly appointed Galileo his court astronomer and mathematician. Philosophers and poets hailed Galileo as a greater discoverer than Columbus, who had only found a new part of Earth, while Galileo had found whole new worlds.

Nothing in *Sidereus nuncius* directly denied the old geocentric, Ptolemaic view of the cosmos or directly promoted the heliocentric, Copernican one. People could still interpret Galileo's finding to mean that the newly found satellites orbited Jupiter while Jupiter revolved around the Earth. Yet the discovery of heavenly bodies that revolved around another planet and not around the Earth had shaken the pillars of the old cosmology. So had Kepler's 1609 book *Astonomia nova* (New astronomy), which set forth two principles that have become known as laws of planetary motion: first, that the planets revolve around the Sun, and that they travel not in circles but in ellipses, or ovals; second, that a planet's speed varies during this orbit, being faster when the planet is near the Sun and slower when the planet is farther from the Sun.

When Kepler read *Sidereus nuncius,* he wrote to Galileo that the discovery of Jupiter's moons supported his own—and Copernicus's—view of the universe. In his reply to Kepler, Galileo tiptoed around the tricky question of whether he believed in the geocentric or the heliocentric cosmology. His next discovery, however, shifted him firmly into the Copernican camp.

Observing Venus in late 1610, Galileo saw that it went through phases like the changing monthly phases of the Moon, from full to dark and back again. The most logical explanation for these changes was that Venus revolved around the Sun, not the Earth, reflecting sunlight as it did so. By then Galileo was certain that the Copernican cosmology was correct. Yet several meetings in Rome in 1611 illustrated the conflict that this knowledge sparked. Galileo met with Church officials, who told him that as a mathematician he could publish his observations, and he could even describe the Copernican system as a mathematical possibility. He could not, however, interpret his observations as fact—in other words, he could not state that the Earth actually moved or that the Sun truly lay at the center of the planets' orbits. But Galileo also attended a dinner given in his honor by the Academy of the Lynx, fellow thinkers who believed that mathematicians and other scientists should be able to present the theories that their observations suggested—in other words, that they had the right to try to explain the world as well as to describe it.

The Linceans, as the members of this group were called, gave Galileo's *perspicillum* a new name: *telescope,* from Greek words meaning "seeing at a distance." In addition, they published a paper Galileo wrote in 1613, describing sunspots and the phases of Venus. It included this sentence: "An understanding of what Copernicus wrote in *Revolutions* suffices for the most expert astronomers to ascertain that Venus revolves about the sun, as well as to verify the rest of his system." Galileo had entered dangerous territory. A few years later the church warned him against believing or defending Copernicanism, but in 1632 he published a work that compared the Ptolemaic and Coper-

GALILEO DEMONSTRATES HIS TELESCOPE, POINTING IT NOT AT THE NIGHT SKY BUT AT THE CITY'S SKYLINE BY DAY. LIKE OTHER EARLY TELESCOPISTS, GALILEO RECOGNIZED THE INSTRUMENT'S POTENTIAL FOR MILITARY USES SUCH AS GETTING A CLOSE LOOK AT AN ENEMY'S FORTRESS OR AN APPROACHING NAVY.

nican systems. Even though Galileo tried to protect himself by noting that he was not claiming to prove the Copernican system, merely to describe it as a mathematical speculation, the book clearly revealed that Galileo favored Copernicanism.

Pope Urban VIII, furious that Galileo had thumbed his nose at earlier warnings from the Church, ordered the aging scientist to stand trial in Rome on the charge of teaching and defending the heretical ideas of Copernicanism after having agreed not to do so. By confessing to "ambition," pleading for mercy, swearing that he did not believe the Earth moved, and promising never to write about Copernicanism again, Galileo escaped Bruno's fiery fate, but he did not escape the Church's wrath entirely. He spent the final decade of his life under house arrest and did no further work in astronomy. Nonetheless, the telescope continued to evolve. Within a few decades, people were gazing at the stars through instruments more powerful—and much, much larger—than Galileo's finest *perspicillum.*

TELESCOPES ARE VITAL TO THE SCIENCE OF ASTRONOMY, BUT THEY CAN ALSO OFFER DRAMATIC VIEWS OF DISTANT OBJECTS ON EARTH, SUCH AS MOUNTAINTOPS.

# Refractors versus Reflectors

The spyglass that Lippershey made and Galileo improved is called—perhaps unfairly—the Galilean telescope. Even though Galileo had made remarkable discoveries with it, this type of telescope had drawbacks. Its field of view, the area that can be seen through the telescope, was small, and each time a more powerful objective lens was used to increase the instrument's magnifying power, its field of view shrank still further. This meant that in order to see more clearly or in greater detail, astronomers had to settle for viewing smaller and smaller pieces of the sky. According to astronomer Fred Watson, studying the heavens through Galileo's thirty-power telescope would have been like looking at the sky through a drinking straw. Yet in spite of the telescope's limitations, Galileo's telescopic discoveries had aroused considerable astonishment. Everyone interested in science or learning wanted one of the new devices—if possible, a better one than anyone else had. Through the efforts of optical experimenters and instrument makers, the Galilean telescope soon gave way to other designs.

The first major improvement to the Galilean telescope came from Johannes Kepler, who had begun explaining the motions of the planets even before Galileo picked up his first *perspicillum*. Although Kepler did not build any telescopes, he described an improved version in a 1611 work called *Dioptrice*. The Galilean telescope had contained a convex objective lens that magnified the image and a concave eyepiece that actually shrank the image but also focused it outside the telescope, near the eye of the observer. Kepler's idea was to replace the concave eyepiece lens with a second convex lens, one that would take the magnified image from the objective lens and magnify it still more. The Keplerian telescope, as this design is called, had a wider field of view than the Galilean. Its main drawback was that the image seen by the observer was inverted, or upside down. Kepler suggested that this problem could be corrected by inserting a third lens into the telescope to invert the image once again, so that it would appear right side up to the observer. Other researchers independently discovered this three-lens arrangment, known as the Keplerian erecting telescope.

People who intended to use telescopes for military purposes or for surveying land preferred the images to be right side up. The Keplerian erecting telescope was well suited for such uses. Some modern terrestrial telescopes today, such as those used by bird-watchers and photographers, incorporate the same basic design.

On the other hand, astronomers did not particularly care whether their images were upside down or right side up. They did, however, want greater magnifying power. Telescope users of the mid-seventeenth century continued to refine the Keplerian telescope by adding more internal lenses—as many as nineteen were reportedly used in one instrument. Increasing the number of lenses, though, meant decreasing the quality of the final image, which was slightly distorted each time it passed through a lens. Lens grinding had advanced since the beginning of the century—glass was purer, surfaces were more accurately shaped, and better polishing techniques removed more blemishes. Still, lenses were less than perfect, and even excellent lenses created two problems: spherical aberration and chromatic aberration.

Spherical aberration occurs when light passes through a lens whose surface is curved in such a way that it is like part of a sphere. Refraction through such a surface produces a blurred image. The problem can be corrected by altering the curve of the lens surface slightly into a form

A NATIVE HUNTER IN THE CANADIAN ARCTIC USES A TELESCOPE TO SCAN THE SURROUNDING ICE AND WATER FOR SEALS.

# Basic Optics: Reflection

A mirror is any smooth, shiny surface that, because it reflects light rays, appears to hold an image of whatever it faces. Mirrors of polished metal were known to all ancient civilizations that practiced metal-working. By Roman times, the art of making mirrors of clear glass with metal backings existed. This art was known in medieval and Renaissance Europe as well, but glass mirrors were expensive and fragile. Most mirrors continued to be made out of metal.

The first to write about the focusing properties of mirrors was an Arabic mathematician and optical researcher named Abu Ali al-Hasan ibn al-Haytham, known in Europe as Alhazen. He pointed out that a mirror with a curved, concave surface would reflect light rays to a focal point, similar to the way a convex lens refracts them to a focal point. A translation of Alhazen's work into Latin, published in 1572, probably encouraged European scientists to consider the possibility of replacing the convex lens of a telescope objective with a concave mirror. Even before the necessary mirror-making technology existed, mathematicians had designed several types of telescopes that combined mirrors with magnifying eyepiece lenses.

Isaac Newton built the first successful reflecting telescope in 1668. Soon other designs appeared. Scottish mathematician James Gregory had actually designed the Gregorian telescope in the early 1660s but was unable to build it. French professor Laurent Cassegrain presented another design in 1672. All three of these compact, efficient telescope designs remain in use today.

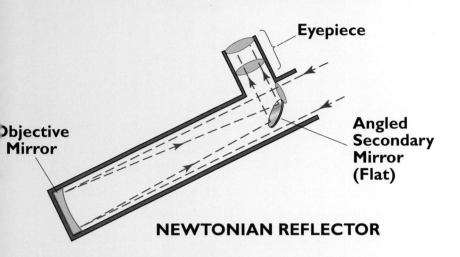

**NEWTONIAN REFLECTOR**

Eyepiece

Objective Mirror

Angled Secondary Mirror (Flat)

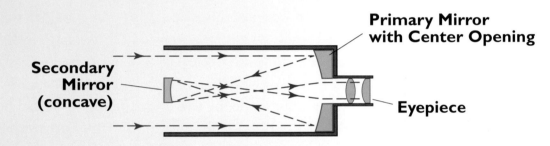

**GREGORIAN REFLECTOR**

Primary Mirror with Center Opening

Secondary Mirror (concave)

Eyepiece

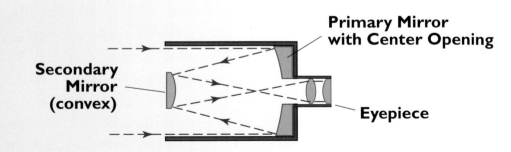

**CASSEGRAIN REFLECTOR**

Primary Mirror with Center Opening

Secondary Mirror (convex)

Eyepiece

Developed in the seventeenth century, these three designs for reflecting telescopes are still used today.

called a hyperboloid, but seventeenth-century lens-making technology could produce only spherical lenses, not hyperboloid ones. Chromatic aberration is a ring or halo of colors around the image. It occurs with lenses of any shape and is caused by the way lenses, like prisms, break white light into a rainbow-like spectrum of different wavelengths.

One way to minimize spherical and chromatic aberration was to use lenses with flatter curves—small segments of a sphere rather than large ones, like an eighth of an orange peel instead of a half. But the shallower, or flatter, the curve of the lens, the longer the len's focal length, and the longer the telescope had to be to accommodate it.

In 1645 a high-quality astronomical telescope was 6 to 8 feet (1.8 to 2.4 meters) long. By 1655 a Dutch astronomer named Christiaan Huygens had built a 23-foot (7-meter), 100-power telescope. With a smaller instrument, Huygens had already discovered Titan, the first of Saturn's moons to be seen. With his new, longer telescope, he solved a problem that had puzzled astronomers since Galileo's time—the question of why Saturn sometimes appeared to be bulging outward in the middle. Some observers had interpreted this bulge as two moons, one on each side of the planet, but Huygens correctly saw that the bulge was a flat disk or ring encircling the planet. (Later astronomers would find that Saturn's ring is really a series of rings separated by gaps.) In addition, Huygens often receives credit for an innovative eyepiece that he attached to his long telescope, although others had worked on it before him. Instead of a single lens like earlier eyepieces, the Huygens eyepiece has two plano-convex lenses placed close together, with both flat surfaces toward the observer's eye. This device enlarged the telescope's field of view and improved the quality of the image.

As stargazers competed to outdo and outview one another, telescopes grew increasingly long, with some instrument makers selling them by the yard. One contestant in this astronomical arms race was Johannes Hevelius, who lived in the city of Gdansk or Danzig on the coast of the Baltic Sea. A brewer by trade, Hevelius was passionate about astronomy and rich enough to build a series of high-quality tele-

A WHIMSICAL IMAGE OF SEVENTEENTH-CENTURY BREWER JOHANNES HEVELIUS, WHO BUILT SOME OF THE LONGEST TELESCOPES OF HIS AGE. LONGER BY FAR THAN THE INSTRUMENT SHOWN HERE, HEVELIUS'S MOST AMBITIOUS TELESCOPES WERE EXTREMELY DIFFICULT TO USE.

scopes. His main contribution to science was publishing the first atlas of the Moon in 1647; it was based on observations made through a 10-foot (3-meter) telescope. Hevelius is most often remembered, however, for his last and longest telescope. With a focal length of 150 feet (45.5 meters), it hung from a mast 90 feet (27 meters) high. It had no tube, simply a V-shaped wooden trough with the objective lens fastened to one end and the eyepiece to the other. Hevelius needed a gang of assistants with ropes and pulleys to maneuver this monster into viewing position, and the tiniest breeze rendered it too shaky to be used.

Huygens also built long, tubeless telescopes like Hevelius's biggest instruments. Those of Huygens, however, lacked even the trough that Hevelius had used to support his lenses. Huygens placed an objective lens in a short metal tube attached to the top of a mast, then sat below and lined up the eyepiece with the objective lens by using a length of taut string. The longest of these constructions had a focal length of 210 feet (64 meters) and was all but impossible to use because of unsteadiness, the lack of a tube to shut out light from nearby sources, and the difficulty of aligning both lenses with the object being viewed. Accounts exist of even longer telescopes being built in the late seventeenth century, but none of them yielded useful observations.

By then the telescope had become a window onto an ever-widening universe. That universe, it was generally agreed, conformed to the Copernican model. Few details were yet known about the planets, however, and astronomers knew nothing about the stars. New and improved telescopes would be needed to carry the Copernican revolution in cosmology forward.

All telescopes up to that time had been refractors, which use a lens as the objective, the part of the telescope that gathers light and focuses an image of the object being viewed. Ever since Galileo, however, mathematicians, astronomers, and instrument makers had discussed using a concave mirror instead of a lens to gather light and focus the image. Because a mirror would reflect light instead of refracting it, chromatic aberration—the ring of color caused by refraction—would not be a problem. In addition, a reflected image would be brighter than a refracted one. But accurately curved mirrors with surfaces smooth enough for telescope use are much harder to make than lenses. Although half a dozen seventeenth-century mathematicians designed reflectors, or telescopes using mirrors as objectives, it was decades before one was successfully built.

The first reflector was the creation of Isaac Newton, professor of mathematics, experimenter with optics, and developer of a theory of gravitation that explained the movements of the planets and other heavenly bodies. Frustrated with chromatic aberration, Newton turned his considerable intelligence and energy to the problem of making a reflecting telescope. First, he needed a suitable mirror. Glass mirrors, made reflective by a thin layer of material such as tin or silver foil, existed, but they were extremely expensive, and glassworkers could not yet make them in the concave shape a telescope required. The majority of mirrors were made of highly polished metal. Newton created his own alloy, or blend of metals: copper, tin, and some arsenic for extra reflectivity. He also developed new methods of polishing the metal to improve the accuracy of the reflection. All of these developments came together in his design for an elegantly simple but

INVESTIGATING THE PROPERTIES OF LIGHT, ENGLISH SCIENTIST ISAAC NEWTON (1643-1727) FOUND THAT ORDINARY WHITE LIGHT BECOMES A RAINBOW OF DIFFERENT COLORS WHEN IT PASSES THROUGH A PRISM.

effective reflecting telescope: a concave mirror to focus the image in the middle of the telescope tube, with a small, flat secondary mirror positioned to direct the image through an opening in the tube, where the observer would view it through the magnifying lenses of a Huygens eyepiece. Newton completed a small model of his reflector in 1668. Several years later, he presented a second reflector to the Royal Society, Britain's leading scientific organization, but he never built a large version or used his invention to study the skies. That work was left for others.

By the end of the seventeenth century, astronomers could choose between two types of telescopes. Each had advantages and disadvantages. Refractors could be more accurate, but they suffered from chromatic aberration. Chester Moor Hall, a British lawyer whose hobby was experimenting with optics, reduced the problem of chromatic aberration in the 1730s by inventing the achromatic lens, which consisted of a convex lens and a concave lens, made of different kinds of glass, close together. The chromatic aberration of the concave lens cancels out that of the convex one, eliminating most of the confusing halo of color from the image. Achromatic lenses soon became standard in telescopes and all other optical instruments. A second problem with refracting telescopes, however, proved more difficult. This was lens sag, the tendency of large glass lenses to become deformed in the center due to the effect of gravity. This meant that refractors would eventually reach a size limit. Large mirrors, in contrast, did not sag because they could be supported by sturdy frames in back, so there was no limit on their size, at least in theory. But the metal mirrors used in telescopes were extremely heavy. In addition, they tarnished and required frequent polishing, which was a time-consuming process during which telescopes had to be disassembled and then reassembled.

Refractors remained in favor for many years. Because their principal advantage was their ability to yield a high-quality, detailed image at high degrees of magnification, they were ideal for studying things that benefited from being enlarged: sunspots, the Moon, planets and other satellites within the solar system. When it came to studying the stars, however, magnification was less important—a point of light remains a point of light even when magnified by the most powerful telescope. For studying objects at stellar rather than solar distances, astronomers needed to gather more light and make images brighter, not bigger. Mirrors could be made much larger than lenses, which meant that reflectors were ideal for astronomers who wanted to study the most distant objects known: the stars. One such astronomer was William Herschel, a German musician living in England. Herschel started observing the skies with refractors that he made himself using purchased lenses and simple tubes of cardboard or cheap metal. He

WITH AN IRON TUBE 40 FEET (12.2 METERS) LONG AND A MIRROR 48 INCHES (1.2 METERS) ACROSS, WILLIAM HERSCHEL'S LARGEST REFLECTOR WAS SUPPORTED ON A ROTATING FRAMEWORK LIKE A TURNTABLE. THE GERMAN-BORN ASTRONOMER, WHO LIVED IN ENGLAND, USED THIS MASSIVE INSTRUMENT BETWEEN 1789 AND 1814. THE TELESCOPE WAS THE SUBJECT OF MUCH INTEREST BY VISITORS, INCLUDING KING GEORGE III, WHO HAD FUNDED ITS CONSTRUCTION.

switched to reflectors in the early 1770s because, as he later wrote, "The great end in view is to increase what I have called the power of extending into space."

Herschel taught himself to cast mirrors of molten metal and produced a series of ever-larger Newtonian telescopes. By 1780 he had made a 20-foot-long (6-meter-long) telescope with a primary mirror that was 12 inches (30 centimeters) across. Herschel made his most famous discovery, however, using an easier-to-manage telescope that was only 7 feet (2.1 meters) long, with a 6-inch (15-centimeter) mirror. Through this instrument in 1781 he spotted a bright moving disk that was soon determined to be an unknown planet. For the first time in history, a new planet—given the name Uranus—had been added to

YERKES OBSERVATORY IN WISCONSIN. THE OPENING IN THE DOME REVEALS THE 40-INCH (102-CENTIMETER) TELESCOPE, THE LARGEST REFRACTOR STILL IN USE IN THE WORLD.

the solar system. Its discovery stunned the scientific world and made Herschel famous, but the astronomer remained more interested in the stars. He devoted the rest of his career to building huge reflectors, the largest of which was 40 feet (12.2 meters) long, with a 48-inch (1.2-meter) mirror that required ten men to move it when it needed polishing. Using these creations, Herschel made two major contributions to stellar astronomy: he discovered that the Sun moves through space, and he determined that the Milky Way is a vast disk-shaped collection of stars that includes the Sun. With this finding, Herschel added the concept of the galaxy to cosmology. He had indeed extended astronomical observation far out into space.

Refracting telescopes got longer and longer as their lenses became more powerful. Reflectors, on the other hand, got fatter and fatter as their mirrors increased in diameter. The fattest reflector of the nineteenth century was called the Leviathan of Parsonstown after Leviathan, a giant beast mentioned in the Bible. Built in 1845 by an Irish astronomer named William Parsons, Lord Rosse, this telescope had a 72-inch (1.8-meter) mirror that weighed 4 tons (3.6 metric tons) and was housed in a tube 8 feet (2.4 meters) across. This massive instrument was the largest telescope in the world. Hung by cables between two stone walls, it gave the brightest views yet of the nebulae, which are glowing clouds scattered among the stars. Parsons discovered that a nebula in the constellation Andromeda appeared to be made up of individual stars. He also found that at least sixty of the several hundred known nebulae had spiral shapes, although the true significance of these "spiral nebulae" would not be known until the 1920s, when they would provide the key to another revolutionary new view of the universe.

The refracting telescope reached its final glory in the second half of the nineteenth century. An American portrait painter named Alvan Clark grew interested in astronomy, taught himself and his sons how to grind lenses, and built a series of high-quality refractors. In 1873 the Clarks installed a telescope with a 26-inch (66-centimeter) lens in the U.S. Naval Observatory in Washington, D.C. Using this telescope, the largest refractor in the world at the time, astronomer Asaph Hall discovered Phobos and Deimos, the tiny moons of Mars. The Clarks also made a 36-inch (91-centimeter) lens for the refractor at the University of California's Lick Observatory and a 40-inch (102-centimeter) one for the University of Chicago's Yerkes Observatory in Wisconsin. The Yerkes refractor saw first light—an astronomer's term for the moment when light first enters a telescope's aperture—in 1897. Still in use, it is the world's largest refractor. An even bigger one, with a lens 4 feet (1.2 meters) across, was built for a world's fair in Paris in 1900. This was the largest refractor ever built, but it was dismantled after the fair for lack of funds to operate it, and no astronomical discoveries were ever made using it.

DOZENS OF NEW ASTRONOMICAL OBSERVATORIES HAVE COME INTO EXISTENCE SINCE THE BEGINNING OF THE TWENTIETH CENTURY. A KEY REQUIREMENT FOR A NEW OBSERVATORY IS A LOCATION THAT OFFERS THE BEST POSSIBLE VIEWING CONDITIONS. IN SEARCH OF DARK SKIES, ASTRONOMERS LOOK FOR PLACES FREE OF LIGHT POLLUTION, THE SPILL OF LIGHT FROM CITIES AND OTHER ARTIFICIAL SOURCES.

# THREE

# Bigger, Better, Brighter

The twentieth century began as the age of the reflector. Big new telescopes revolutionized our knowledge of the universe by giving astronomers their first views of evolving galaxies. The century also brought new emphasis on astrophysics, a science that explores all of the physical properties of astronomical bodies through telescopes that collect radio waves and infrared radiation as well as visible light. Observatories sprang up in places with dark skies and clear air, in deserts and on mountaintops, but still astronomers yearned for more light-gathering ability. By the end of the century they were using a Very Large Telescope (VLT) and were dreaming of an Overwhelmingly Large Telescope (OWL), one whose highly advanced optics and computer technology would let them see farther into the universe than ever before.

Several technological developments in the nineteenth century paved the way for the big reflectors and astronomical discoveries of the twentieth. One of these developments concerned mirror making. In the 1850s, inventors in France and Germany found ways to manufacture high-quality glass mirrors coated with silver film. Telescope builders soon found that a large silver-on-glass mirror weighed a third as much as a metal mirror of the same size and collected twice as much light because of its higher reflectivity. The metal mirror became

THE MARRIAGE OF ASTRONOMY AND PHOTOGRAPHY ALLOWED BOTH PROFESSIONAL AND AMATEUR ASTRONOMERS TO CAPTURE IMAGES THROUGH THEIR TELESCOPES. THE CAMERA ATTACHED TO THIS TELESCOPE IS ACTIVATED BY A HAND-HELD CABLE RELEASE. THE TELESCOPE SITS ON A TRIPOD WITH AN EQUATORIAL MOUNT, A MOTORIZED DEVICE THAT MOVES THE TELESCOPE TO TRACK THE MOVEMENT OF THE STARS ACROSS THE SKY.

a thing of the past. By the 1930s, the silver coating on telescope glass had been replaced by aluminum, which remains more reflective because it is less likely to tarnish.

Photography was another nineteenth-century invention that helped shape modern astronomy. In 1840 an American chemist and amateur photographer named Henry Draper made the first known astronomical photograph by aiming his camera at the Moon for twenty minutes. As photographic equipment and techniques improved over the following decades, astronomical photography also advanced, yielding images of solar eclipses, sunspots, and thousands of stars. Photography offered astronomers several key advantages. First, a photograph is a permanent record, more accurate than a drawing, that can be consulted again and again. Second, a camera attached to a telescope can see more than an astronomer looking through the same telescope can ever hope to see. Unlike a human eye, a camera can build up a cumulative image over time, as long as its aperture remains open—in other words, as long as the film or other recording medium is exposed to light. A long-exposure photograph captures faint elements and details that would otherwise remain forever invisible to the eye.

The first time Galileo turned his telescope toward familiar constellations, he was startled to see hundreds of new stars in them. Similarly, astronomer David Gill, after photographing a comet in 1882, was surprised to see scores of new stars in the background of the photograph. They had been invisible to him when he took the picture, but the camera had brought them into view. Five years later, a group of astronomers launched an international campaign to make a new map of the entire sky based on photographs. Mechanical developments accompanied the rise of astronomical photography. Tracking—keeping a telescope pointed at its target for the duration of the exposure, while the target moved slowly across the sky—was essential, and instrument makers rose to the challenge with motorized mounts that could move a telescope at the precise speed without jarring the device and ruining the image.

The first major reflecting telescopes of the new century were the work of two Americans, the eccentric but dedicated astronomer George Ellery Hale and the skilled telescope builder George Willis Ritchey. Hale was one of the inventors of the spectroheliograph, a device for photographing the Sun, and had overseen the building of the Yerkes Observatory, with its large refractor. Determined to build an even larger reflector, he acquired a 60-inch (1.5-meter) piece of glass for Ritchey to make into a telescope mirror. By this time, telescopic equipment was extremely expensive. It had to be housed in a protective structure that allowed access to the sky, usually through a revolving domed roof with an opening in it. Elaborate structural supports were required to support the weight of large telescopes, which needed exact alignment and tracking equipment as well as superior optics. Individual astronomers could no longer build and maintain top-quality private observatories. Instead, the big telescopes were funded by universities, foundations, or generous philanthropists. It was the Carnegie Institution that paid for the installation of Hale's 60-inch (1.5-meter) reflector at Mount Wilson, a California observatory Hale had founded for solar observations. Eleven years later, in 1917, Hale and Ritchey unveiled Mount Wilson's second large reflector, the 100-inch (2.5-meter) Hooker Telescope, named for the Los Angeles businessman who paid for the mirror. With these two telescopes, astronomers would answer some of the most pressing astronomical questions of the early twentieth century.

Ever since Herschel, astronomers had recognized that the Earth's solar system is part of a huge disk-shaped community of stars called a galaxy. Herschel had called the galaxy an "island universe." He and most other astronomers assumed that the solar system was located near the center of the galaxy, but the galaxy's dimensions were not known until American astronomer Harlow Shapley joined the staff at Mount Wilson in 1914. Shapley used the 60-inch (1.5-meter) Mount Wilson reflector to study the globular clusters. These bright, ball-shaped groups of stars are unevenly distributed in the sky. Most are near the constellation Sagittarius, which is crowded with stars. In the opposite direction, the much emptier constellation Auriga has very few globular clusters. Shapley speculated that the globular clusters were distributed around the center of the galaxy, which would place the center off in the direction of Sagittarius. After measuring the distances to certain bright stars in the globular clusters, Shapley concluded that the galaxy was bigger than anyone had thought, so big that it would take light 300,000 years to cross it, traveling at about 6 trillion miles (10 trillion kilometers) a year. Furthermore, announced Shapley, the solar system was located not in the center of the galaxy but toward one edge of it.

Shapley was right about the position of the solar system but wrong about the size of the galaxy. He overestimated it because he did not realize that he was viewing the center of the galaxy through clouds of gas and dust that interfered with his measurements. The galaxy is now known to be about 100,000 light-years across, with the solar system about 26,000 light-years from its center. The Milky Way, the band of light across the night sky that gives the galaxy its name, is the dense population of stars we see when looking through the length of the disk-shaped galaxy.

Shapley was wrong about something else, too. In a 1920 debate sponsored by the National Academy of Sciences, he argued that the Milky Way galaxy was the entire universe. Another astronomer, Heber Curtis from the Lick Observatory, countered that the Milky Way was just one of many galaxies in a vastly larger universe. At the heart of the debate were the astronomical objects called nebulae.

Nebulae, whose name comes from the Latin word for "cloud," had puzzled astronomers for several centuries. Herschel had counted about 2,500 of these glowing clouds and noticed that they seemed to be of several types. Some appeared to contain stars; others looked as if they were made of gas. Herschel suggested that the starry nebulae might be "island universes" like our own galaxy. In the mid-nineteenth century, Irish astronomer William Parsons discovered with his Leviathan telescope that

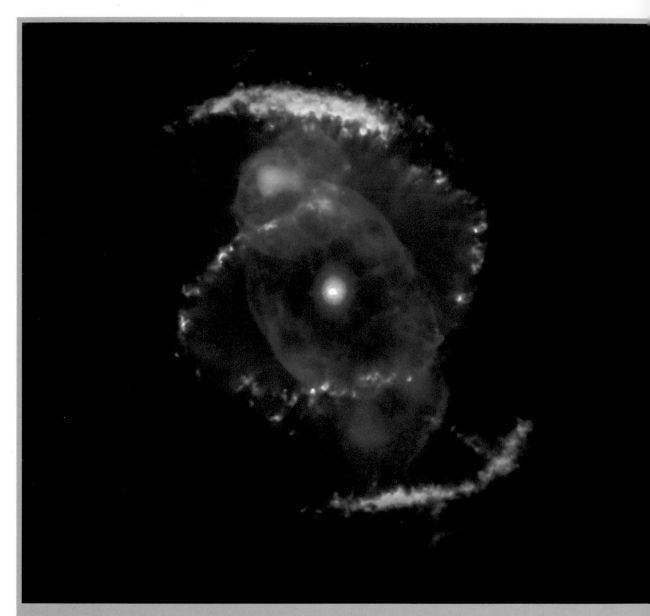

SWIRLS OF GLOWING GAS GIVE NEBULA NGC6543 ITS POPULAR NAME: THE CAT'S EYE NEBULA. THIS GAS CLOUD IS THE WRECKAGE OF A DYING STAR ABOUT THREE THOUSAND LIGHT-YEARS FROM EARTH. TELESCOPIC OBSERVATION EXPLAINED THE NATURE OF NEBULAE, ONE OF THE BIG PUZZLES OF EARLY MODERN ASTRONOMY.

many nebulae were spiral in shape. By that time British astronomer William Huggins had proved that about a third of all nebulae were gas clouds. But what about the others—especially the spiral-shaped ones that looked like huge collections of stars? Could they be distant galaxies? Some leading astronomers of the early twentieth century thought that suggestion was nonsense; others found it increasingly convincing. By the time of the 1920 debate, astronomical opinion was divided on whether the spiral nebulae were star formations within the Milky Way or other galaxies outside it.

The 100-inch (2.5-meter) Hooker Telescope and astronomer Edwin Hubble would settle the question. Hubble spent several years photographing two bright spiral nebulae through the telescope. Using the same method as Shapley—locating bright stars of a known type whose distance could be calculated—Hubble found that these nebulae lay far outside the boundaries of the Milky Way galaxy. As he announced in 1924, they had to be separate galaxies. Hubble spent the next few years surveying hundreds of nebulae. He found that many of them were galaxies, arrayed at different distances from the Milky Way. Not all were spiral; some were shaped like balls or flattened ovals. From that time on, the term *nebula* referred only to clouds of gas and dust within the Milky Way. The bodies formerly called starry or spiral nebulae were acknowledged to be galaxies.

Hubble's discovery brought another huge shift in thinking about cosmology, or the structure of the universe. Astronomers recognized that Milky Way was just one of many galaxies in a universe larger than anyone had previously imagined. It also inspired Hale to begin work on an even larger telescope, a 200-inch (5-meter) reflector to be established atop Mount Palomar in California. Hale died in 1938, but work continued on the instrument, which was completed ten years later and named the Hale Telescope. It was the largest and most advanced telescope of its time and remains a major tool for astronomical research today. By the time it was completed, however, new kinds of telescopes were becoming available to serve the science of astrophysics.

USING A LONG EXPOSURE, A PHOTOGRAPHER HAS MADE THE DOME OF THE MOUNT PALOMAR OBSERVATORY SEEM TRANSPARENT, REVEALING THE GIANT HALE TELESCOPE INSIDE. THE HORSESHOE-SHAPED STRUCTURE IS PART OF THE MOUNTING THAT SUPPORTS THE TELESCOPE AND ALLOWS IT TO BE POINTED AT VARIOUS SECTIONS OF THE SKY.

Astrophysics is the study of all of the physical properties of the planets, stars, and other heavenly bodies: their chemical makeup, temperature, density, and so on. Traditional astronomy, which uses optical telescopes to observe and photograph the skies, is part of astrophysics, but astrophysicists have other tools as well. The first of these, the spectroscope, was invented in the nineteenth century. In 1814 a German spectacle maker named Joseph Fraunhofer noticed that when he passed sunlight through a telescope and then through a prism, the light fanned out into a pattern of more than five hundred vertical lines, some thick and dark, others thin. During the 1850s, German scientists identified these Fraunhofer lines as representing specific chemicals, each with its own distinctive pattern. A spectroscope, which is an instrument containing a prism, can be used in a laboratory to identify materials. If the spectroscope is attached to a telescope, however, it can be used to identify the chemical components of a celestial body. Suddenly astronomers had access to an entirely new kind of information. William Huggins had used a spectroscope in the 1860s to determine that gaseous nebulae contain hydrogen. He wrote, "So unexpected and important are the results of the application of spectrum analysis to the objects in the heavens, that this method of observation may be said to have created a new and distinct branch of astronomical science."

Spectroscopy was well established as part of astronomy by the early twentieth century. Like traditional astronomy, it uses visible light—the same light waves that are perceived by the human eye, by optical telescopes, and by the ordinary camera. Visible light consists of light waves with a range, or spectrum, of different wavelengths, from violet, which has the shortest wavelength, to red, which has the longest. But visible light makes up only 2 percent of the electromagnetic spectrum, which is the full range of all energy waves in the universe. Infrared rays, microwaves, and radio waves have longer wavelengths than visible light; ultraviolet rays, x-rays, and gamma rays have shorter wavelengths. Just like visible light, these wavelengths carry information about bodies in space. Astronomers simply needed the right equipment to detect it. Beginning in the mid-twentieth century, astrophysicists developed tools to gather information from these other parts of the electromagnetic spectrum.

In 1931 Karl Jansky became the first to collect some of this invisible information from space. Jansky was no astronomer. He was an engineer at Bell Telephone Laboratories in New Jersey, and he was trying to solve a problem: a faint, persistent, mysterious hiss that interfered with Bell's new transatlantic telephone service, which carried phone messages on radio waves. Jansky attached a set of radio antennas to a rotating framework mounted on wheels from a Model T Ford and set it turning, hoping to pinpoint the source of the annoying static. The hiss, however, seemed to come from everywhere at once. Jansky eventually determined that it was loudest in the direction of Sagitarrius, toward the center of the Milky Way, where stars are thickest. This "background noise" proved to be radio waves emitted by the stars themselves. A few years later, a radio engineer named Grote Reber built a large antenna in the form of a dish-shaped parabola, the shape that astronomers had found was best for gathering and concentrating light waves. For six years, Reber aimed his homemade antenna—really a radio telescope—at the night sky. At the end of that time he had made the first radio map of the Milky Way galaxy.

After World War II ended in 1945, radio astronomy took a great leap forward, in part because a lot of surplus wartime radio equipment became available to experimenters and observatories. In 1957 Jodrell Bank Observatory began operation in England. It had the world's first large, steerable radio telescope, a dish 250 feet (76 meters) across. Six years later, a 1,000-foot (300-meter) version was set up at Arecibo, Puerto Rico. Since then, radio astronomers have concentrated not on building larger dishes but on creating arrays—chains of independent radio telescopes that can work together to yield the same result as a single enormous one. For example, the Very Large Array (VLA) radio telescope in New Mexico has twenty-seven movable dishes, each of them 82 feet (24.8 meters) across.

Radio astronomy brought a series of cosmological revelations. Radio astronomers determined that the Milky Way is a spiral galaxy, like the nearby Andromeda galaxy and many others. Researchers also discovered that galaxies rotate. But an accidental discovery in the next-longest range of wavelengths, microwave radiation, helped solve one of the biggest scientific puzzles of the century: the origin of the universe.

In 1929 Edwin Hubble had discovered that not only is the universe full of galaxies, they are moving away from one another at tremendous speed. To many astrophysicists, this suggested that the universe is expanding from an initial event that came to be called the Big Bang. According to this theory, all matter and energy were once compressed into an infinitely dense, small globe. The universe came into existence

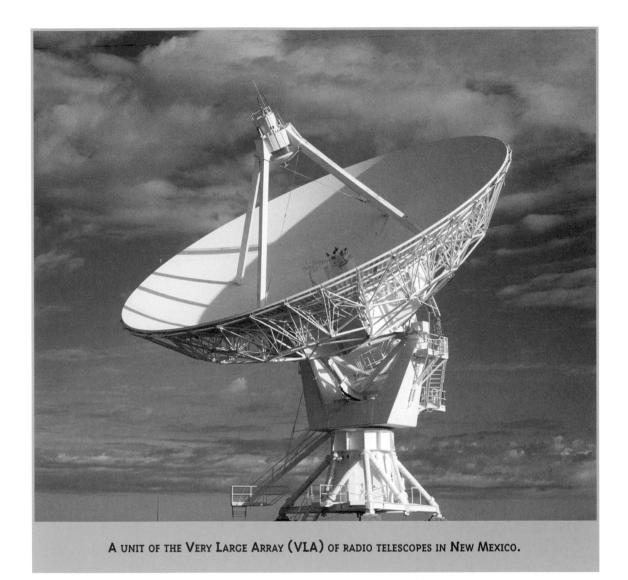

A UNIT OF THE VERY LARGE ARRAY (VLA) OF RADIO TELESCOPES IN NEW MEXICO.

at the moment when this grapefruit-sized mass expanded, an explosive event that scattered matter and energy outward in all directions. Some astrophysicists criticized the Big Bang theory, pointing to a lack of evidence. Confirmation of the theory came from an unexpected source. In 1964 two Bell Labs engineers were testing a new, sensitive type of antenna that was to be used for communicating with satellites in the microwave range of radiation. Just as had happened more than three decades earlier with the radio antenna, they were troubled by a mysterious, inescapable hiss. Soon physicists and engineers working together had identified the hiss as microwave radiation in the exact frequency that would correspond to residual energy from the Big Bang, "noise" left over from the birth of the cosmos. This cosmic background radiation, as it is called, gave significant support to the Big Bang theory, which the majority of cosmologists now accept.

As the twentieth century continued, universities and national science foundations in many countries either built new astronomical observatories or added to existing ones. Seeking locations that offered the best conditions for seeing the sky, astronomers gravitated to mountains and deserts, areas with clear air and little humidity. Good sites were also located far enough from large population centers to escape light pollution in the night sky. Several major late-twentieth-century observatories, some for optical astronomy and others for radio astronomy, were constructed in the American Southwest, Australia, the Andes Mountains of Chile, the Canary Islands, and Hawaii.

A major modern optical observatory is likely to have several telescopes of different sizes and for different purposes. In addition to a large reflector, it might have a smaller Schmidt reflector, a type of telescope developed in the 1930s that is ideal for photographing large sections of the sky; it can capture an entire constellation in a single image. An observatory will probably also have spectroscopes, spectrographic imaging devices, and an infrared camera or even a telescope dedicated to observations in the part of the infrared spectrum that is closest to visible light. This near-IR spectrum, as it is called, is good for studying relatively cool items in space, such as giant red stars. Astronomers photograph the farther infrared spectrum, more remote from visible light, to study things such as clouds of gas and dust. Radio astronomy also remains important. In 1995, the United States and Mexico began a joint venture to build a 165-foot (50-meter) radio telescope on Sierra Negra, one of Mexico's highest mountains. Able to detect extremely short radio waves, the telescope will be used to create new and more detailed maps of the early galaxy as it existed thirteen billion years ago.

During the 1970s and 1980s, eight telescopes of around 13 feet (4 meters) in diameter were built around the world. Although small compared with the giants of earlier decades, these scopes were of high quality. More important, they were combined with a new type of imaging equipment called the charge-coupled device (CCD). A CCD is a set of light-sensitive photoelectric cells that can capture more light than photographic film or plates. CCDs were first used for astronomical photography in 1975, when a trio of astronomers used one of the new devices to capture an image of Uranus. Highly accurate and digital in format, CCDs have now largely replaced cameras in astronomy.

The desire for ever-bigger telescopes persisted. A new generation of giants appeared to eclipse the Hale Telescope, which had been the world's largest for almost three decades. In 1975 that title went to a 238-inch (6-meter) reflector at the Russian site of Zelenchukskaya. Plagued with problems ranging from poor optics to the turbulent weather of the Caucasus Mountains, this instrument has never lived up to its potential, although for about twenty years it was the biggest reflector in the world.

The Keck I and Keck II telescopes at Mauna Kea, Hawaii, completed in 1993 and 1996, each measure 394 inches (10 meters) across. They marked an important innovation in telescope design. Instead of consisting of a single large mirror, each of the Keck scopes is made up of thirty-six independently mounted hexagonal mirrors arranged together like the cells in a beehive. The result is a telescope with four times the magnifying power of the 200-inch (5-meter) scope at Palomar. Astronomers have used the Keck telescopes in recent years to study, among other things, the massive stellar explosions known as supernovas and to locate dozens of planets in other solar systems.

Computers made the innovative design of the Keck telescopes possible. Connected to sensors and control mechanisms built into the tel-

THE KECK I AND KECK II TELESCOPE DOMES SIT ATOP MAUNA KEA, A 13,796-FOOT (4,180-METER) EXTINCT VOLCANO IN HAWAII. ABOVE THEM IS COMET HALE-BOPP, NAMED FOR THE AMATEUR AND PROFESSIONAL ASTRONOMERS WHO SIGHTED IT AT THE SAME TIME IN 1997. ITS BLUE TAIL IS IONIZED GAS; THE WHITE ONE CONSISTS OF DUST GRAINS.

escope, computers control and monitor the movement of the hexagonal mirrors, making hundreds of tiny adjustments each second to ensure that the segments work together so smoothly that the collection of thirty-six individual mirrors has the same effect as a solid mirror. Other kinds of computer programs and applications have become essential to astronomy. One is active optics, a set of software commands that controls a telescope's supports, adjusting them as needed to keep the telescope from becoming distorted by its own weight or by changes in temperature. Another set of commands, called adaptive optics, monitors atmospheric conditions and automatically adjusts the focus of a telescope for the best possible imaging. Computers have also made possible a new way of using telescopes, both radio and optical, called interferometry. This is the simultaneous use of several separate instruments to yield a more detailed and accurate result than any of them could provide independently. A computerized process called aperture synthesis combines the data from many different telescopes to give the effect of a single much larger instrument. In a version called very long baseline interferometry (VLBI), precisely timed images from telescopes at locations thousands of miles apart are synthesized, or combined. The result is an image that appears to have come from a single enormous telescope rather than from many separate instruments.

The largest individual telescopes in the world are the two Keck scopes and the similarly sized Southern African Large Telescope (SALT), which became operational in late 2005 and has a segmented mirror like those of the Kecks. Interferometry, however, has created an even larger "virtual telescope" at the European Southern Observatory in Chile. This aptly named Very Large Telescope (VLT) consists of four 323-inch (8.2-meter) reflectors that can be used independently. When combined through interferometry and aperture synthesis, however, they become the equivalent of a 630-inch (16-meter) telescope. The VLT has produced spectacular images of remote objects such as the Horsehead Nebula, a dark cloud that astrophysicists believe is a "nursery" where stars are formed. In 2005 it was used to observe something closer to home: Comet 9P/Tempel 1 after it was struck by a research probe. The VLT was able to produce images of the fan-shaped impact site.

Construction is under way at several sites around the world on other large telescopes with segmented mirrors, but some astronomers and telescope designers have already leaped ahead, designing what they hope will be the next generation of super-large instruments. The most ambitious example is the Overwhelmingly Large Telescope (OWL), which would have 3,048 segments forming a mirror 3,937 inches (100 meters) in diameter.

If OWL is ever built, one thing is certain. Like the Kecks and other recently constructed telescopes, it will lack one thing that telescopes had for hundreds of years: a human observer. Even a telescope as big as the Hale instrument at Mount Palomar, intended primarily to photograph the sky, had an observation platform where an astronomer could actually look through the telescope. The newer instruments, however, are designed to capture images with CCDs. An astronomer using one of the cutting-edge modern telescopes does not bend over an eyepiece,

THE PRIMARY MIRROR OF THE HOBBY-EBERLY TELESCOPE AT THE MCDONALD OBSERVATORY IN TEXAS, MADE OF NINETY-ONE HEXAGONAL SEGMENTS, DOES NOT HAVE TO MOVE TO TRACK OBJECTS ACROSS THE SKY. INSTEAD, A FEW FOCUSING INSTRUMENTS SUSPENDED ABOVE THE MIRROR DO THE TRACKING, REDUCING THE AMOUNT OF MASS THAT MUST BE MOVED DURING A NIGHT OF OBSERVATION BY MORE THAN TEN TIMES.

peering through a tube. He or she sits in a control room—possibly even in an office far from the site of the telescope—monitoring a computer screen or downloading the results of a night's viewing from a database.

Old-fashioned eye-to-eyepiece observation still takes place around the world, however. Many older or smaller telescopes at universities and observatories operate in the traditional way. Backyard astronomy thrives, too. Every night, people somewhere point home telescopes or even binoculars at the sky, marveling at craters on the Moon or the glowing gas cloud of a nebula. Sometimes, as they watch the sky, they see a tiny speck of light moving across it in a measured orbit—one of the satellites that have carried telescopes to new heights.

THE HUBBLE SPACE TELESCOPE, PLACED IN ORBIT AROUND THE EARTH IN 1990, WAS NOT THE FIRST TELESCOPE IN SPACE, BUT IT IS THE BEST KNOWN. AMERICAN ASTRONOMER NEIL deGRASSE TYSON HAS CALLED IT "THE WORLD'S MOST FAMOUS MIRROR."

# Telescopes in Space

Nicolaus Copernicus, the mathematician who forever changed humankind's understanding of its place in the universe, died more than half a century before telescopes were invented and four centuries before people began sending rockets into space. So he might have been amazed—though perhaps honored—to see his name attached to a metallic object, looking something like an oversized silver refrigerator with wings, that was launched into orbit around Earth in 1972. Copernicus was one of the first satellites to carry a telescope into space.

In the early days of rocket science, a few people dreamed of sending telescopes into space. A telescope above Earth's atmosphere would avoid many of the problems of earthbound astronomy. One such problem is light pollution from growing cities and other sources. Another is weather—the biggest, costliest, most cutting-edge optical telescope is not much use on a cloudy night. Even on clear nights, though, temperature variations, winds, and airborne particles cause vibration and turbulence in the various layers of the atmosphere, which is why the stars appear to twinkle when seen from Earth. By building observatories high in the mountains, above as much of the atmosphere as possible, and by using adaptive optics, astronomers can minimize the effects of turbulence, but they cannot escape it entirely.

The rise of astrophysics brought another reason to consider space-borne telescopes. When scientists became aware that all wavelengths of the electromagnetic spectrum carry information about the universe, they also realized that much of that spectrum is blocked, or absorbed, by the Earth's atmosphere. Visible light is, of course, visible. Radio waves are easily detected. Part of the infrared (IR) spectrum can also be perceived on Earth, especially by telescopes at high altitudes. In 2004, for example, the VLT in the Andes Mountains yielded the first infrared pictures of a planet in another solar system. But most of the ultraviolet, x-ray, and gamma-ray wavelengths cannot penetrate Earth's atmosphere. To make full use of these wavelengths, scientists would have to send their instruments into space.

In 1946 an American astrophysicist named Lyman Spitzer, Jr. wrote a report for the U.S. government describing the kinds of research that could be carried out by a telescope above the atmosphere. At the time, rocketry was still developing and space travel was a distant prospect. The possibilities of high-altitude astronomy were clear—scientists had already studied the Sun's ultraviolet spectrum using instruments sent aloft on a V2 rocket. But, as J.B. Zirker reports in *An Acre of Glass: A History and Forecast of the Telescope* (2005), "Spitzer's report was probably filed and forgotten until 1957, when the Russians launched Sputnik and the U.S. government was shocked into action." Alarmed by the Russians' advance into space, Congress established the National Aeronautics and Space Administration (NASA) to oversee American space exploration. In the following years, most public attention focused on missions involving astronauts, but NASA also sent many telescopes into space, sometimes in cooperation with the space agencies of other nations.

By 1975 NASA had sent eight observatories into orbit to record astrophysical information about the Sun and other high-energy radiation sources. The best known was Skylab, which during its nine-month mission in 1973 studied the corona, the Sun's luminous outer atmosphere. NASA also launched Orbiting Astronomical Observatories

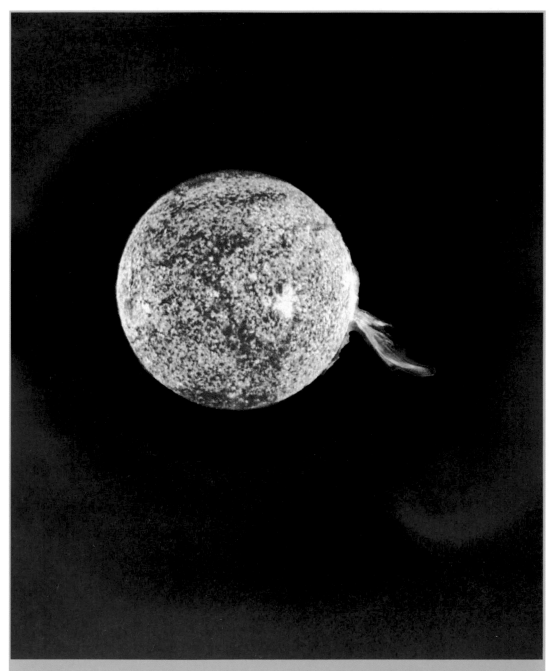

PHOTOGRAPHED IN ULTRAVIOLET LIGHT FROM THE ORBITING OBSERVATORY SKYLAB IN 1973, A BUBBLE OF SUPERHEATED GAS IS EJECTED FROM THE CORONA, THE HOT OUTER PART OF THE SUN'S ATMOSPHERE.

(OAOs), telescope platforms designed for studying the stars. Between 1968 and 1973, the first successful OAO made thousands of stellar observations through ultraviolet telescopes. Copernicus, the second successful OAO, was equipped with both x-ray detectors and an ultraviolet telescope. For nine years it fed astronomers new data about stars and clouds of interstellar gas and dust. In 1978 NASA, the United Kingdom, and the European Space Agency (ESA) launched the International Ultraviolet Explorer (IUE), which for eighteen years produced a stream of discoveries, including spots on stars (believed to be similar to the sunpots on the Sun), auroras on Jupiter, and winds emitted by young stars.

A year before the launch of the IUE, the U.S. Congress approved funds for the large space telescope that Spitzer had described decades earlier. The LST, as planners called it, would be closely linked to NASA's shuttle program, which had created reusable spacecraft to carry astronauts to and from orbit around Earth. Years of planning and construction followed, and not everything went as project managers hoped. Problems building the 94-inch (2.4-meter) mirror delayed progress, which in turn led to the omission of some tests during the final stages of manufacturing. The LST was originally scheduled to be launched in 1983 but was not ready. By 1986 the satellite—which had been christened the Hubble Space Telescope (HST) in honor of the American astronomer who had identified the spiral nebulae as galaxies—was set to be carried into space by a shuttle crew, but the disastrous explosion of the shuttle *Challenger* grounded the entire shuttle fleet for more than two years and drastically slowed NASA's space program. Not until 1990 did the shuttle *Discovery* release the solar-powered HST, equipped with CCDs, computers, and an array of navigation and communication equipment, into its orbit 381 miles (613 kilometers) above Earth. For the next month, the telescope's NASA controllers struggled with start-up problems, including a balky telescope cover and difficulty keeping the satellite steady, that had to be solved before Hubble could see first light.

Back on Earth, astronomers eagerly awaited the first images from the new space telescope. When they finally arrived, however, the images were blurred by spherical aberration. The edges of Hubble's primary mirror, it turned out, had been ground incorrectly. Its curve was off by about one-fiftieth the diameter of a typical human hair. Aside from its spectrographs, which operate independently of the optical mirror to investigate the chemistry of the universe, the $1.5 billion space telescope was useless.

NASA bore the weight of much criticism and ridicule—American humorist Dave Barry, for example, called Hubble "the only space telescope with dark glasses and a cane." Fortunately, engineers were able to develop a package of optics that, when installed in the satellite, would correct the problem. After intensive training, the astronauts of the shuttle *Endeavour* carried out the eleven-day repair mission in 1993. Once again astronomers held their breaths, waiting for pictures—and this time they were not disappointed. Hubble started producing a stream of remarkable images that have excited astrophysicists and, thanks to the Internet, thrilled people all over the world.

Some large land-based telescopes, such as the Kecks, can see farther into space than Hubble. The great advantage of Hubble is that it sees more clearly. In addition to photographing objects and events in the solar system, such as the crash of the comet Shoemaker-Levy into the planet Jupiter in 1994, Hubble has produced some of the most useful images ever made of what astrophysicists call deep space—the far reaches of the visible universe. Before the HST, astrophysicists speculated about black holes, collapsed stars with gravitational fields so powerful that even light is sucked into them. They could not, however, confirm the existence of black holes through ground-based observation. By measuring the speed of gases being drawn into these gravitational wells, however, the HST has provided good evidence for the existence of black holes and supermassive black holes, one of which is now thought to be at the center of the Milky Way galaxy.

The HST has also photographed the births and deaths of stars, collisions between distant galaxies, and the ejection of glowing matter from a supernova, the closest such stellar explosion to Earth in the past four hundred years. And although scientists have known since the time of Edwin Hubble that the universe is expanding, astrophysicists who used the HST to measure the distances to a number of galaxies have made the closest estimate yet of its rate of expansion—and therefore of the age of the universe, which they believe to be about fourteen billion years. They also know something about how the universe looked in its first billion years of life, thanks to two studies called the Hubble Deep Field (1995) and the Hubble Ultra Deep Field (2004). For these studies, the HST's telescope was

focused at a tiny patch of sky for a long time, until a great amount of light had been gathered. The resulting images reveal the most distant objects ever seen: galaxies thirteen billion light-years away. Their light traveled for thirteen billion years before being captured by the telescope, which therefore looks far back in time as well as across space. Astrophysicists are still studying these images, which include galaxies in shapes never before seen, to discover what they might reveal about how galaxies formed in the early stages of the universe's expansion.

Hubble was the first in a series of four space tele-

ASTRONAUT F. STORY MUSGRAVE APPROACHES THE HUBBLE SPACE TELESCOPE DURING THE 1993 SERVICING MISSION. AFTER THE ASTRONAUTS ATTACHED ADDITIONAL LENSES TO CORRECT A FLAW IN THE MIRROR, HUBBLE YIELDED FLAWLESS IMAGES, INCLUDING SOME OF THE BEST AVAILABLE INFORMATION ABOUT DEEP SPACE.

scopes that NASA calls the Great Observatories. The second, the Compton Gamma Ray Observatory, was launched in 1991 and re-entered the Earth's atmosphere in 2000. Its mission was to study violent, high-energy processes such as collisions between stars or galaxies. The Chandra X-Ray Observatory, placed in orbit in 1999, observes objects such as black holes and supernovas in the x-ray range of the electromagnetic spectrum, using the smoothest mirrors ever produced and optics with a focusing power equivalent to the ability to read a newspaper at a distance of half a mile (0.8 kilometer). In 2003 NASA launched the fourth and final Great Observatory, the Spitzer Space Telescope, which is the largest infrared telescope ever sent above the atmosphere. Astrophysicists are using it to study regions of space blocked from optical view by dust and gas clouds, as well as to investigate dim stars and planets outside the solar system.

By 2005, after four missions to repair or update its equipment, the Hubble Space Telescope was still producing excellent images. Its future is uncertain, though, because funding may not be available for further maintenance. Still, its ground-based controllers intend to keep it operating as long as possible. Meanwhile, NASA, the European Space Agency, and other groups have launched a host of additional space telescopes, including instruments to map the cosmic background radiation and to study the mysterious explosive events called gamma-ray bursts. The European Space Agency is designing Darwin, a project that will use interferometry to link several orbiting satellites into an array that designers hope will be large enough to spot and study Earth-sized planets revolving around other stars. NASA, meanwhile, is building the next generation of space telescope, one that will be launched sometime around 2013 to replace Hubble. Dubbed the James Webb Space Telescope in honor of an early NASA administrator, it will have a 20-foot (6.5-meter) mirror. It is being designed especially for infrared observations of the oldest galaxies and stars, those that formed soon after the Big Bang, when the universe was in its infancy.

WHILE THE TELESCOPE EXTENDED HUMAN SIGHT INTO OUTER SPACE, THE MICROSCOPE—INVENTED AROUND THE SAME TIME—USED THE SAME LENSES AND OPTICAL PRINCIPLES TO REVEAL THE SECRETS OF EVERYDAY THINGS, SUCH AS THIS ANT'S HEAD MAGNIFIED TWENTY-SEVEN TIMES.

## ⟿ F I V E ⟾

# Exploring the Microworld

Microscopes were invented around the same time as telescopes—probably a few years earlier. But in the years and centuries that followed, they generally aroused less public excitement. Even today, no microscope has the widespread and instant recognition of, say, the Hubble Space Telescope. Yet microscopes have undoubtedly touched more people's lives, intimately and directly, than telescopes have. For while telescopes opened humankind's eyes to the universe, microscopes led to a growing understanding of life itself—and the diseases that threaten it. In the hands of biologists, bacteriologists, scientific researchers, and medical workers, microscopes yielded discoveries that ultimately saved countless lives.

The early histories of the microscope and telescope are very similar. Both instruments originated in the spectacle shops of the Netherlands. Both were made and used by many of the same people. They even acquired their names from the same source. The Linceans, the members of the Roman Academy of the Lynx, came up with the term *telescope* to describe the device that Galileo had made for seeing objects at a distance. Galileo also produced a few of the new magnifying instruments for seeing small things close at hand in greater detail than was possible for the naked eye. He marveled at the sometimes startling perspectives that these instruments offered on the world, writing, "I have seen flies which look as big as lambs." In 1624 Galileo presented one of these instruments to the Linceans. Using *telescope* as a model, a member of the academy coined the name *microscope* from the Greek words for "seeing small."

At first, the microscope magnified things about nine times, at best, and people regarded it as little more than a curiosity. By the mid-seventeenth century, however, experimenters across Europe were improving the instruments and carrying out systematic research with them. Around 1660, for example, an Italian named Marcello Malpighi was using a microscope when he discovered capillaries, the tiny blood vessels that link veins and arteries, and thus proved the controversial theory that blood circulates between them. But the two most dedicated and skilled of the early microscopists were a versatile English genius named Robert Hooke and a keen-eyed Dutch tradesman named Antoni van Leeuwenhoek. Together they laid the foundations of microscopic science.

Born in 1635, Hooke attended Oxford University, where he gained a reputation for his skill in building scientific equipment and designing experiments. For the rest of his life Hooke was both an experimenter and an inventor, active in a number of fields, including astronomy, chemistry, physics, and architecture. In 1662 the newly formed Royal Society of London appointed him its curator, which meant that it was his reponsibility to demonstrate, or at least to report on, one or two new scientific experiments each week. He did so faithfully until his death in 1703; he also taught geometry at Gresham College in London, collaborated with architect Christopher Wren in the rebuilding of the city after the Great Fire of 1666, made some of the first scientific studies of weather, and discovered the Great Red Spot on the planet Jupiter. Among Hooke's many inventions are the universal joint, the respirator, the ear trumpet, the sash window, and a machine for measuring wind strength. Hooke is most often remembered, however, for his first major book, which he published when he was thirty years old. Called *Micrographia: Or Some Physiological Descriptions of Minute Bodies Made By Magnifying Glasses,* the book not only showed how microscopy could be applied to biological study but also provided detailed instructions for making and using microscopes.

Hooke constructed a number of microscopes over the years. His tube-shaped instruments were of a type now known as the compound light microscope, which has a light source and at least two lenses—an objective lens to magnify the image of the specimen and an ocular, or eyepiece, to further magnify and focus it. Hooke's later microscopes employed the double-lensed ocular called the Huygens eyepiece that had already come into use for telescopes. In addition, Hooke invented a lamp specifically to serve as a light source for microscopy. It consisted of a candle and a water-filled glass that served as a movable lens to focus the candlelight onto the specimen he was examining. One of his most important contributions to microscope design was the iris diaphragm, a screen with a central opening surrounded by retractable segments. By manipulating a lever that caused these segments to draw together or pull apart, the operator could shrink the central opening or enlarge it. Hooke modeled this construction on the iris of the eye, which contracts and dilates around the pupil; the same design is still used on the apertures of microscopes and cameras.

The best of Hooke's microscopes magnified objects thirty times. Yet as Hooke realized, magnification is only half of what a microscope's optics must do. The other important part of a microscope's performance is its resolving power, or resolution, which refers to the minimum distance between two points on the specimen that can be seen through the microscope as separate points rather than as a single undifferentiated or blurred surface. An average hu-

WORKING FROM DETAILS IN ROBERT HOOKE'S *MICROGRAPHIA*, A MODERN INSTRUMENT MAKER RECONSTRUCTED THE TELESCOPE THAT THE PIONEERING SEVENTEENTH-CENTURY MICROSCOPIST USED TO MAKE REVOLUTIONARY DISCOVERIES. THE ILLUMINATION SYSTEM WAS A LIQUID-FILLED GLASS GLOBE THAT PROJECTED THE LIGHT FROM A FLAME ONTO THE SPECIMEN BEING EXAMINED.

man eye, for example, can resolve two objects that are 0.1 millimeters apart. Resolution in a microscope depends on lens quality, and although Hooke was a good lens grinder, the materials available to him meant that he had to settle for less-than-perfect lenses and images that were often blurry. Still, with patience and skill he managed to perform hundreds of detailed microscopic studies. And Hooke, who had begun training as an artist before he entered the university, recorded his observations in the magnificent, highly accurate engravings that illustrate *Micrographia.*

Among the specimens that Hooke examined under his microscope—and demonstrated to his scientific colleagues at the Royal Society—were feathers, sponges, and moss. Like Galileo, he looked at insects, including a flea, whose shell-like segmented outer covering he described as "a curiously polish'd suite of sable Armour, neatly jointed." When Hooke looked through his microscope at a thin slice of cork, which is a tree bark, he wrote, "I could exceedingly plainly perceive it to be all perforated and porous, much like a Honey-comb, but that the pores of it were not regular." Hooke added that "these pores, or cells . . . were indeed the first *microscopial* pores I ever saw, and perhaps, that were ever seen, for I had not met with any Writer or Person, that had made any mention of them before this." Hooke used the word *cell* because the tiny compartments in the cork reminded him of the small compartments, or cells, within a monastery. With that sentence he named the structural unit of living matter, the basis of cellular biology.

As he explored the mysteries of the natural world through his microscope, the practical and inventive Hooke was inspired by many of the things he saw magnified for the first time. Bees' stingers and the stinging hairs on nettles made him envision a hollow, pointed needle for injecting solutions into people—the first recorded idea of the hypodermic syringe. When he studied a silkworm's fine threads, he speculated that perhaps artificial silk could be made by spinning a gluelike substance into thread, much as polyester fabric is made today. One of Hooke's inspirations led him to an invention: Noticing that the bristles on an oat grain shrank and stretched with changes in the humidity, he developed the hygrometer, an instrument to measure the moisture content of air.

*Micrographia* was a best-seller. Some readers mocked Hooke for having spent a fortune on microscopic equipment, only to waste his time looking as such seemingly insignificant things as mites and the peels of plums. Most, however, were fascinated by the window Hooke had opened to an unseen dimension of everyday life. Samuel Pepys, a government official whose diary is an illuminating account of life in seventeenth-century London, stayed up until 2 a.m. reading *Micrographia* and called it "the most ingenious book that ever I read in my life." And some readers did more than admire Hooke's work. Motivated by *Micrographia,* they built or bought microscopes and started their own research. One of these individuals was Antoni van Leeuwenhoek of Delft, in the Netherlands.

Leeuwenhoek, who came from a humble family of basket makers and brewers, worked as a fabric merchant, surveyor, and city official. Although he attended school as a child, he received no higher education; instead he studied on his own the subjects that most interested him. Sometime before 1668, after reading *Micrographia,* he became a diligent microscopist.

He started by learning to grind lenses so that he could build a microscope. Leeuwenhoek eventually became an extremely skilled lens grinder who specialized in making very small biconvex lenses with steep curves—big, but smooth, outward bulges on each side. With magnifying powers that ranged from fifty to more than two hundred, these were the most powerful microscopic lenses of the time. They also had remarkable resolving power; the best

SELF-TAUGHT AND INTENSELY CURIOUS, ANTONI VAN LEEUWENHOEK BECAME THE FINEST MICROSCOPE MAKER IN EUROPE. HE WAS THE FIRST TO DISCOVER LIVING ORGANISMS THAT WERE INVISIBLE TO THE UNAIDED EYE.

of them could resolve details down to one micrometer (a micrometer, sometimes called a micron, is one-millionth of a meter, equal to 1/25,000 of an inch). The steep curvature of Leeuwenhoek's lenses gave them a very short focal length, which meant that the image was focused close to the lens. This in turn meant that Leeuwenhoek's eye had to be within about a millimeter of the lens to use the microscope. Although Leeuwenhouk mounted these lenses in several different types of microscopes, he most often used a style of his own design—a simple but effective microscope that was really a glorified magnifying glass. The lens was mounted in a paddle-shaped brass frame, about the size of the palm of a hand, that Leeuwenhoek could bring close to his eye to make his observations. Attached to the paddle was a spike that could hold a specimen. Screws moved the spike back and forth, and toward and away from the lens, for focusing. Leeuwenhoek made hundreds of microscopes, although only a handful survive. His creations were less complex than the compound instruments Hooke and other early microscopists were using, but they were the finest of their day, with superb, clear lenses. They were also easy to use—at least for Leeuwenhoek, who, modern experts believe, must have had keen eyesight at close range.

In 1673 a Dutch scientist wrote to the secretary of the Royal Society in London, praising Leeuwenhoek's excellent microscopes and his research. The secretary then wrote to Leeuweehoek, inviting him to share his discoveries, beginning a remarkable correspondence that continued for fifty years, until Leeuwenhoek's death. The Royal Society published around two hundred of Leeuwenhoek's letters, making the work of the Dutch microscopist—who never wrote a scholarly paper or published a book—available to the world. Leeuwenhoek could not draw, so he hired an artist to illustrate the specimens he observed and described. Leeuwenhoek's observations were so accurate, and his directions to the artist were so clear, that modern biologists instantly recognize most of the illustrated specimens.

Like Hooke, Leeuwenhoek studied a wide variety of specimens: sand, fossils, even gunpowder. Most fascinating to him, however, were biological specimens, especially the many different kinds of tiny living organisms he discovered through the microscope. Leeuwenhoek called them "animalcules."

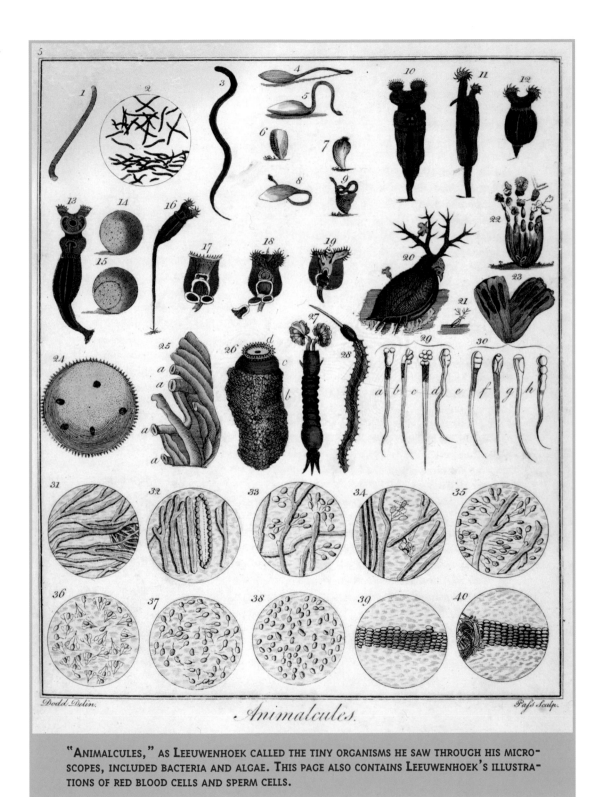

*Animalcules.*

Dodd Delin.

Pass Sculp.

"ANIMALCULES," AS LEEUWENHOEK CALLED THE TINY ORGANISMS HE SAW THROUGH HIS MICRO-
SCOPES, INCLUDED BACTERIA AND ALGAE. THIS PAGE ALSO CONTAINS LEEUWENHOEK'S ILLUSTRA-
TIONS OF RED BLOOD CELLS AND SPERM CELLS.

Leeuwenhoek's interest in animalcules began in 1674, when he looked at a drop of lake water and saw green globules and several different kinds of free-swimming things that he realized had to be alive. He was looking at protists, members of a large and varied category of minute life-forms that includes algae (the green globules), protozoa (the tiny swimmers), and, smaller still, bacteria. When Leeuwenhoek sent word of the animalcules to England, Robert Hooke copied Leeuwenhoek's microscope design as closely as he could and used the resulting instrument to confirm Leeuwenhoek's find. After that, the two men became correspondents; Hooke once wrote to Leeuwenhoek that most of the serious work in microscopy was being done by the two of them. After Leeuwenhoek had shown the way, other microscopists discovered protozoa, but Leeuwenhoek saw and described more kinds—and smaller ones—than anyone else. He seems to have felt almost affectionate toward these tiny creatures, such as the *Vorticella,* a type of water-dwelling protozoon he described in a 1702 letter: "In structure these little animals were fashioned like a bell, and at the round opening they made such a stir, that all the particles in the water thereabout were set in motion thereby." He went on to say that he found the "gentle motion" of their tails "mightily diverting."

Squeamishness did not prevent Leeuwenhoek from looking for life everywhere. Examining plaque scraped from his teeth, he saw "many very little living animalcules, very prettily a-moving." What he had found were living bacteria; Leeuwenhoek was the first to see them. In true scientific fashion, he sought a wider sample, looking for plaque-dwelling bacteria from his wife and daughter—and from two old men who had never cleaned their teeth. He found it. He also discovered still more bacteria, as well as parasitic protozoa, living in a specimen of his feces. In other studies, Leeuwenhoek was the first to see red blood cells and live sperm cells. In addition, he discovered several kinds of microscopic worms and pioneered techniques of microdissection that allowed him to study the insides of insects as small as aphids.

Because the Royal Society circulated reports of Leeuwenhoek's discoveries, always giving him full credit, the Dutch microscopist became widely

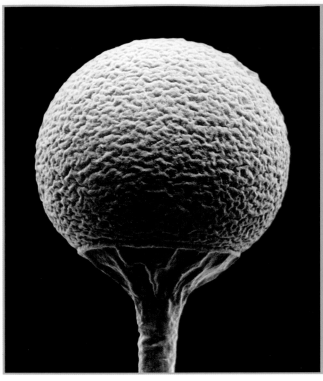

THE SPORE OF A BREAD MOLD IS SO TINY THAT IT IS ALMOST INVISIBLE, BUT THE MICROSCOPE REVEALS ITS STRUCTURE AND SURFACE FEATURES. MICROSCOPISTS' GROWING UNDERSTANDING OF NATURE'S HIDDEN STRUCTURES AND PATTERNS WOULD EVENTUALLY TRANSFORM MANY FIELDS OF SCIENCE, INCLUDING MEDICINE.

known. In his later years he received a steady stream of letters and visitors from admirers and fellow scientists. Although he was happy to have his discoveries recognized, he wrote in 1716 that his work "was not pursued in order to gain the praise I now enjoy, but from a craving after knowledge, which I notice resides in me more than in most other men."

In their own way, the early microscopists brought about a revolution in knowledge as profound as the new cosmology of Copernicus and Kepler. They showed the world that there is, quite literally, more to life than meets the eye. Although a few ancient philosophers had speculated that the matter we see around us is made up of some kind of invisibly small particles, people had not seriously considered the possibility that everything around them consisted of structures and parts whose organization existed just below the threshold of sight. The microscope lifted the veil and revealed these hidden patterns. Especially revolutionary were the discoveries that all living things—including people—share certain microscopic features such as cells, and that all living things are inhabited by smaller forms of life. Just as Copernicus and Kepler took the first huge steps toward placing the Earth and the solar system in their true relationship to the universe, Hooke and Leeuwenhoek led the way toward an understanding of humankind's relationship to the rest of the natural world.

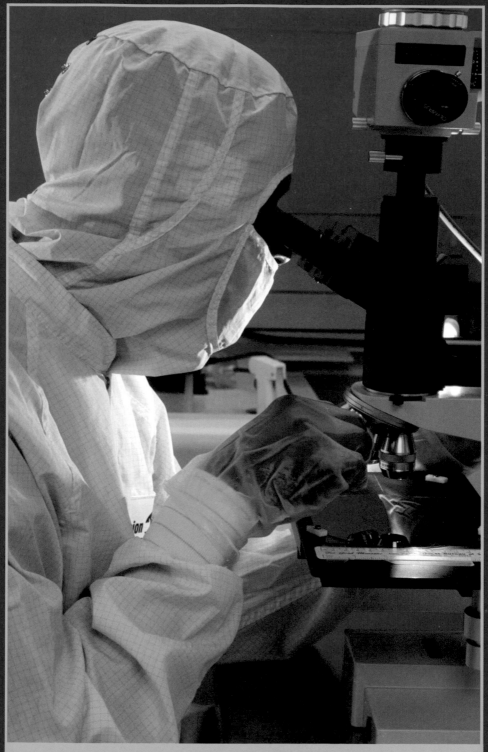

MICROSCOPES ARE WOVEN INTO MODERN LIFE IN COUNTLESS WAYS. BEYOND THEIR USES IN SCIENTIFIC RESEARCH AND MEDICINE, THEY ARE AN ESSENTIAL PART OF MANY INDUSTRIES. HERE A TECHNICIAN USES A MICROSCOPE TO INSPECT NEWLY MANUFACTURED COMPUTER CHIPS.

# From Germs to Atoms

Pioneers such as Hooke and Leeuwenhoek established the microscope as a scientific tool, just as Galileo had demonstrated the scientific merits of the telescope. Like the telescope, the microscope has evolved since those pioneering days. First, inventors, optics researchers, physicists, and engineers improved and refined the microscope Hooke knew. Then, in the twentieth century, other innovators created new types of microscopes altogether. Even Hooke's fertile, inquiring mind might not have been able to imagine the uses people have found for these powerful instruments, from solving crimes and curing diseases to reattaching severed limbs and mapping the surfaces of atoms.

Although Leeuwenhoek's handheld microscopes were superior to Hooke's because of their excellent lenses, it was Hooke's design—a standing tube through which the microscopist looks down at the specimen—that became standard. That design, the compound light microscope, is still common today. The microscopes that students use in biology classes, as well as most microscopes for home and amateur use, are of this type, although they incorporate many features and materials unknown to Hooke.

One of the first refinements to Hooke's basic telescope was a tray called the stage. Attached to the telescope frame beneath the base and the objective lens, the stage holds the specimen for viewing. A hole in

MADE IN 1765 IN BELGIUM, THIS ORNATE BRASS MICROSCOPE HAS ALL OF THE BASIC FEATURES OF THE COMPOUND LIGHT MICROSCOPE, INCLUDING A STAGE TO HOLD THE SPECIMEN AND A MOVABLE MIRROR TO REFLECT LIGHT.

the stage allows light to pass from the light source through the specimen, illuminating it. Hooke's light source was a candle focused through a glass of water. Later microscopists used a small pivoting mirror, mounted on the base of the microscope, to reflect light upward through the specimen. Some telescopes still come with mirrors; others have built-in lamps with adjustable brightness.

Some of the most important advances in microscope technology involved lenses. Like the double-lensed Huygens eyepiece, many of these advances applied equally to microscopes and telescopes. In an age when science had not yet become highly specialized, science-minded researchers pursued their interests in multiple fields, and some individuals—including Huygens and Hooke—built and used both telescopes and microscopes. Lenses in both kinds of instruments shared similar problems. Chromatic aberration created halos of fuzzy color. Spherical aberration, or blurring of the edges of the image, was most troublesome with the highly curved lenses that yielded higher powers of magnification. When Chester Moor Hall invented the achromatic objective lens in the 1730s to reduce the problem of chromatic aberration in telescopes, he also improved microscopy. Not until 1830, however, did microscopists receive help with spherical aberration. In that year an optical experimenter named Joseph Jackson Lister reported that with the right combination of microscope lenses properly spaced in a row, the first len's aberration is cancelled out by the lenses behind it. This led to the development of compound or multi-part objective lenses.

As the new art and science of photography took shape in the mid-nineteenth century, it held the same attraction for microscopists as it had for telescopists. They knew that they could capture what they saw through the eyepiece more accurately with a photograph than with a drawing. A number of people, working independently around the same time, developed ways of combining the camera and the microscope. One of the most influential was Joseph J. Woodward, an assistant surgeon in the Union army during the American Civil War. As a pathologist charged with studying diseased tissues, Woodward learned how to use the microscope, and from an astronomer who had created a tele-scopic camera he got advice on how to turn his microscope into a camera by replacing the eyepiece with a photographic plate. Instead of looking at the specimen he created a picture of it. In this way Woodward produced more than a hundred slides for a book on the medical and surgical history of the war; he also developed synthetic dyes for use in staining specimens so that their details would appear with sharper contrast. Woodward's work helped make the camera, used together with the microscope, a valuable tool in studying disease. Photographs of micro-

IN 1830 JOSEPH JACKSON LISTER—SHOWN HERE WITH ONE OF HIS MICROSCOPES—FOUND AN ARRANGEMENT OF LENSES THAT ELIMINATED SPHERICAL ABERRATION, THE BLURRING THAT HAD PLAGUED GENERATION OF MICROSCOPISTS.

scopic specimens gradually replaced illustrations in textbooks. Many microscopes today are equipped with digital cameras or even video-recorders.

Taking pictures of specimens viewed through a microscope is called photomicroscopy, or sometimes photomicrography. Its opposite, microphotography, involves using a microscope in reverse: projecting a normal-sized image through a microscope, from the eyepiece toward the objective, so that a minute version of the image appears on the microscope slide. If the slide has been coated with photographic chemicals, it captures the image and can then be developed just like a photograph, producing a slide bearing a tiny picture that can only be seen through a microscope. During the nineteenth century, microphotography became a fad among some microscope hobbyists. They presented each other with such gifts as miniaturized poems or copies of famous paintings that appeared to be mere blobs to the unaided eye but revealed their secrets through the microscope. Like photomicroscopy, however, microphotography had serious uses. As early as 1870, armies used it to make microscopic secret messages that pigeons could carry during wartime. By the mid-twentieth century, advances in microphotography had produced the data storage system called microfilm, as well as the microdot, a piece of film the size of a period that could hold a miniaturized text. Microphotography later developed into photoreduction, the process by which miniaturized circuits are etched onto computer chips.

As the quality of microscope lenses improved during the nineteenth century, so did magnification and resolution, the twin measurements of a microscope's power. By the mid-nineteenth century, microscopists and physicists wondered: How small can we go? Would ever-better lenses make it possible to keep seeing the microworld in ever-finer detail, or was there a limit to the amount of detail that could be seen even with the best possible microscope? German mathematician Ernst Abbe answered that question in 1872. Deeply interested in optics, especially in the challenges of microscopy, Abbe had gone into partnership with lens maker Carl Zeiss to form the Zeiss Optical Works. As research director of the company, Abbe devoted himself to perfecting the microscope. First, he and Zeiss developed a better way to illuminate specimens. They added a new optical component to the telescope, between the light source and the stage where the specimen is mounted. Now called a condenser, this apparatus consists of two lenses, one of which is mounted on an adjustable frame so that the distance between them can be adjusted. With the condenser, which also includes an adjustable iris diaphragm, a microscopist can focus the light flow to illuminate the specimen with either a wide or a narrow beam of light.

Abbe's next contribution clarified the relationship between magnification and resolution. In theory, a microscopist could increase magnifying power indefinitely by stacking lenses, using more and more of the strongest possible objectives and eyepieces in one long compound lens arrangement. In practice, though, it doesn't matter how much magnifying power a microscope has if the person using the instrument cannot resolve, or clearly distinguish, points on the specimen. Magnification that exceeds the instrument's resolving power is useless. Abbe used his knowledge of mathematics and optics to calculate the smallest resolution possible, based on the wavelength of light. This physical limit to resolution is about 0.2 micrometers, or 200 nanometers (a nanometer is a unit of microscopic measurement equal to one-billionth of a meter). Abbe and Zeiss set out to produce microscopes that could reach that limit. Through consultations with glassworkers and experimentation, they discovered methods of mixing batches of better-quality glass for lensmaking. Abbe designed a new type of objective lens, the apochromat, that combined ten or more different convex and concave lenses, made of different formulations of glass, to perfectly align red, yellow, and blue light for better control of chromatic aberration. He also developed a technique called oil immersion, which uses a special objective lens to view the specimen through a drop of clear oil, enlarging the image. With these enhancements, Abbe was able to resolve images to the limit of possibility.

While nineteenth-century mathematicians, optics experts, and microscope makers advanced the technology and techniques of microscopy, researchers in biology were using microscopes to gain greater insight into what makes living organisms tick—and what makes them sick. Using the improved achromatic microscopes available by the second half of the century, researchers could observe things smaller than any seen before, such as previously unknown kinds of bacteria and other microbes, or microorganisms. The result was a new theory of disease and several new branches of medical science: microbiology and bacteriology.

Over the centuries, scientists and physicians had developed many theories to explain how infectious diseases such as smallpox and influenza entered the human body and passed from one person to another. French chemist Louis Pasteur eventually found the true explanation, although he started by investigating the causes of problems in beer brewing. He made microscopic studies of fermentation, a chemical transformation brought about by yeast as part of the brewing process, and in the 1850s he discovered that fermentation is brought about by the activities of certain microorganisms—in other words, yeast is alive. Despite vigorous opposition from scientists who found Pasteur's claim both outlandish and distasteful, Pasteur was able to prove it with carefully designed experiments. By the early 1860s he had proved that similar microorganisms exist in ordinary air. A few years later, he proved that a disease that affects silkworms is caused and transmitted by specific bacilli, which are a type of rod-shaped bacteria. With this discovery, Pasteur established the germ theory of disease, which referred to disease-causing microbes in general as germs.

Pasteur's findings inspired Scottish surgeon Joseph Lister (son of Joseph Jackson Lister, the optical experimenter who had conquered the problem of spherical aberration in the 1830s) to develop antisepsis, an entirely new approach to hospital and surgical procedures that required equipment to be sterilized in order to avoid exposing patients

FRENCH BIOLOGIST AND CHEMIST LOUIS PASTEUR (1822-1895) DISCOVERED THROUGH EXPERIMENT AND MICROSCOPIC RESEARCH THAT ORGANISMS HE CALLED GERMS ARE THE TRUE CAUSE OF MANY DISEASES. HIS NAME LIVES ON IN THE PROCESS CALLED PASTEURIZATION, ONE WAY TO REMOVE HARMFUL MICROBES FROM FOOD.

## TYPICAL COMPOUND LIGHT MICROSCOPE

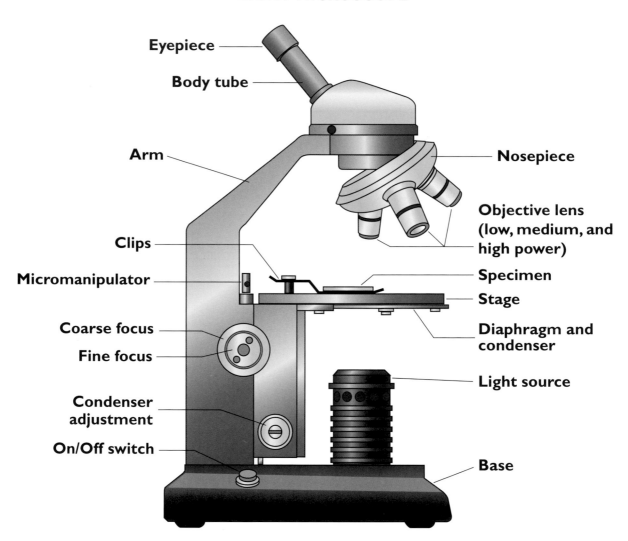

Eyepiece

Body tube

Arm

Nosepiece

Objective lens (low, medium, and high power)

Clips

Specimen

Micromanipulator

Stage

Coarse focus

Diaphragm and condenser

Fine focus

Condenser adjustment

Light source

On/Off switch

Base

THE INSTRUMENT HAS BECOME MORE SOPHISTICATED AND EASIER TO USE, BUT THE BASIC ELEMENTS OF THE COMPOUND LIGHT MICROSCOPE WOULD BE RECOGNIZABLE TO EARLY MICROSCOPIST ROBERT HOOKE. THIS TYPE OF MICROSCOPE IS WIDELY USED TODAY BY STUDENTS AND HOBBYISTS.

to microbes. In addition, once Pasteur had discovered that microbes cause infectious disease, he and other scientists working in the new field of bacteriology turned to their microscopes to isolate the causes of particular illnesses. In Germany, Robert Koch found the bacilli responsible for tuberculosis and cholera. Soon researchers had identified the specific microorganisms that cause many of the world's most widespread and serious diseases. This led to the development of vaccinations against these diseases as well as improved treatments for illnesses. The discoveries of these late-nineteenth-century microbiologists and bacteriologists had revolutionized the medical approach to infectious disease; the line of research they started continues today as microbiologists study the processes of living cells and seek cures for diseases such as colds, influenza, and AIDS.

The evolution of the compound light microscope continued, too, as inventors produced new forms of the instrument. One was the stereo microscope, which has two complete optical tubes, one for each eye, giving the microscopist a three-dimensional view of the specimen. Another was the phase contrast microscope, invented in 1932 by Dutch physicist Frits Zernike. It applies the principle of diffraction, which is the slight bending of light waves as they pass around an edge. The results of this slowing, called phase contrast, cannot be seen, but Zernike discovered that if he inserted a diffraction grating—a plate of glass with fine grooves on its surface—into the microscope between the objective and ocular lenses, the phase contrast is amplified and becomes visible. This advance let scientists study living cells for the first time. To view a transparent specimen such as a cell through an ordinary microscope, a scientist must first dye or stain the specimen to reveal its internal structure through contrast. Dyeing kills the specimen, but the phase contrast microscope, for which Zernike won the Nobel Prize in Physics in 1953, allows colorless biological specimens to be viewed without dyeing. It also advanced the study of mineral and metal samples. Such samples formerly had to be coated with acid to highlight their surface structure, but the phase contrast microscope let scientists view them without the acid treatment.

Another type of light microscope is the fluorescence microscope, used to study specimens that can be made to fluoresce, or emit light when light strikes them. Some materials fluoresce naturally, but many others can be treated with dyes that cause fluorescence. In a fluorescence microscope, the specimen itself becomes the light source. Light from another source is aimed at the specimen to create fluorescence; the microscopist then observes the fluorescing specimen. This technique is extremely useful in biomedical research because it illuminates specimens and parts of specimens that are normally invisible, even through phase contrast microscopes.

While optical experimenters made advances in scientific microscopy, science-fiction writers in the first half of the twentieth century created their own imaginative uses for microscopes. Some of them combined microscopy with current ideas about the structure of atoms, which were then thought to resemble the solar system, with a nucleus at the center, like the Sun, and electrons whirling around it like planets. If atoms were like solar systems, these writers speculated, could our solar system be an atom in some much vaster universe? Or, looking in the other direction, could an atom in our universe be a tiny solar system?

Ray Cummings explored these ideas in his 1922 novella *The Girl in the Golden Atom.* The story opens as the narrator tells his friends how he became obsessed with microscopy: "'I secured larger, more powerful instruments. I spent most of my money,' he smiled ruefully, 'but never could I come to the end of the space into which I was looking. Something was always hidden beyond—something I could almost, but not quite, distinguish.'"

With help from "one of the most famous lens-makers of Europe," the narrator creates a "vastly more powerful" lens and builds a new microscope. Gazing through it at his mother's wedding ring, he sees a beautiful girl. Finally he realizes that he is seeing into an atom in the ring, and that the girl is an inhabitant of that microscopic world. He explains to his friends, "'I believe that every particle of matter in our universe contains within it an equally complex and complete universe, which to its inhabitants seems as large as ours. I think, also, that the whole realm of our interplanetary space, our solar system and all the remote stars of the heavens are contained within the atom of some other universe as gigantic to us as we are to the universe in that ring.'" To which one of his listeners replies, with complete appropriateness, "'Gosh!'" As the story unfolds, the narrator—an ingenious inventor—creates a device to shrink himself down into that atomic world so that he can meet his golden dream girl.

Cummings's idea was entertaining, but it was much more fiction than science. Even a "vastly more powerful" super-lens would be subject to the laws of optics that, as Ernst Abbe had shown, set a limit on resolution. No one would ever see an atom, much less its interior, using an instrument that depended on lenses and light waves. To see an atom, scientists would have to invent a new kind of microscope altogether. Nine years after Ray Cummings published his tale of atomic adventure, they did.

German physicists Max Knoll and Ernst Ruska constructed a microscope that passed streams of electrons, instead of light waves, through a specimen or across its surface. Instead of optical lenses, the electron microscope had magnetic coils that acted like lenses, bending and focusing the electron streams. And instead of an eyepiece, the electron microscope had a camera that could record the image created by variations in the streams. The first images Ruska made with this new device were of the surfaces of gold and copper specimens. The instrument, he discovered, had a magnifying power of ten, about the same as a microscope made in the 1590s, or Galileo's *occhialino* from a few decades later. It took several centuries for the light microscope to reach its full potential, but the electron microscope advanced much more rapidly.

In 1933 Ruska unveiled an improved electron microscope that broke Abbe's optical-lens limit, resolving images at less than 200 nanometers. The following year, the electron microscope was used for

# ELECTRON MICROSCOPES

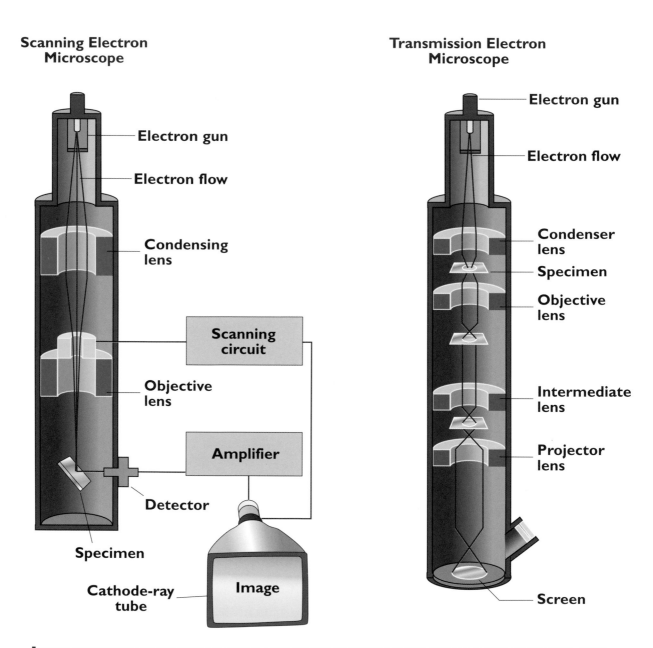

**Scanning Electron Microscope**

- Electron gun
- Electron flow
- Condensing lens
- Scanning circuit
- Objective lens
- Amplifier
- Detector
- Specimen
- Cathode-ray tube
- Image

**Transmission Electron Microscope**

- Electron gun
- Electron flow
- Condenser lens
- Specimen
- Objective lens
- Intermediate lens
- Projector lens
- Screen

INSTEAD OF PASSING LIGHT THROUGH A SPECIMEN, THE ELECTRON MICROSCOPE PASSES STREAMS OF THE TINY PARTICLES CALLED ELECTRONS ACROSS ITS SURFACE. IN PLACE OF LENSES, AN ELECTRON MICROSCOPE HAS MAGNETIC COILS TO BEND AND FOCUS THE STREAMS. THE SCANNING ELECTRON MICROSCOPE (SEM) PRODUCES A HIGHLY DETAILED THREE-DIMENSIONAL IMAGE OF AN OBJECT'S SURFACE BY BOUNCING THE BEAM OFF IT. THIS CREATES A PATTERN OF ELECTRONS THAT IS SCANNED, AMPLIFIED, AND SENT TO A MONITOR, WHERE IT FORMS AN ELECTRONIC IMAGE OF THE SPECIMEN. IN CONTRAST, THE TRANSMISSION ELECTRON MICROSCOPE (TEM) SENDS THE ELECTRON BEAM THROUGH A VERY THIN SLICE OF A SPECIMEN TO REVEAL ITS INTERNAL STRUCTURE.

the first time on a biological sample, the leaf of a sundew plant. The specimen had been fixed, or coated with a fine metallic film, to enhance the contrast of its features. This practice is followed in much electron microscopy today. Ruska's invention quickly became a commerical product; by 1939, a German manufacturer was offering electron microscopes for sale. Then electron microscopy took a leap forward in the 1950s, when several new, extremely fine cutting and slicing tools—the ultramicrotome and the diamond knife—became available. With these tools, microscopists could prepare biological specimens as thin as 200 angstroms (an angstrom is a unit of microscopic measurement equal to one-tenth of a nanometer, or one ten-billionth of a meter) for viewing.

Electron microscopes today fall into two main categories developed in the mid-twentieth century: the scanning electron microscope (SEM) and the transmission electron microscope (TEM). In a scanning electron microscope, a focused electron beam from a moving probe sweeps across the surface of the specimen, which is often fixed with gold, platinum, or some other substance to heighten contrast. The electron beam excites electrons on the surface of the specimen and knocks some of these electrons from the specimen. These freed electrons form the image. In a transmission electron microscope, the electron beam passes through the specimen, revealing its internal structure. The TEM has been especially useful for biological research into the structure and function of the various parts of cells. Both the SEM and the TEM produce images on viewing screens. These images, which are in black and white, are often enhanced with computer-added color to make them easier to interpret.

The wavelengths of electrons are several thousand times shorter than the wavelengths of visible light, which means that electron microscopes can achieve resolutions several thousand times greater than light microscopes. With resolution possible down to 0.2 nanometers, electron microscopists can produce images of specimens magnified by as much as a million times, and these images can be photographically enlarged for

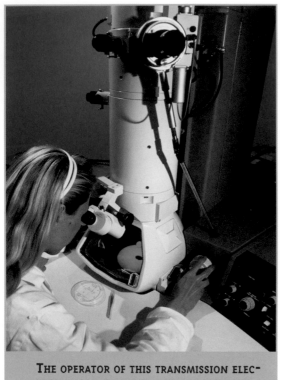

THE OPERATOR OF THIS TRANSMISSION ELEC-TRON MICROSCOPE PEERS INTO A MAGNIFY-ING DEVICE THAT IS ATTACHED TO THE SCREEN WHERE THE ELECTRONIC IMAGE OF THE SPECIMEN APPEARS. SHE USES THE MAGNIFIER TO IMPROVE HER VIEW OF THE IMAGE ON THE SCREEN, WHICH MAY HAVE A RESOLUTION OF UP TO FOUR HUNDRED TIMES BETTER THAN THAT OF A SCANNING ELECTRON MICROSCOPE.

even greater magnification. The resolution and magnification properties of the electron microscope have opened new horizons in biomedical research. For example, scientists can now see and study viruses, which are smaller than bacteria—as much as a million times smaller, in some cases. Other highly specialized types of microscopes, however, can go even further. In 1951 Erwin Müller of Germany became the first person to see an individual atom. He used a new instrument he had invented, the field ion microscope. With the instrument, the specimen—which must be metal—is formed into an extremely sharp tip, cooled to super-low temperatures, and then inserted into a chamber filled with a gas such as helium or neon. When an electric charge is applied to the tip, the tip repels the nearby ions of the gas. Their movements, recorded on a sensitive detector, create an image of the atoms on the surface of the tip. The field ion microscope has been used to study the atomic structures of many metals. But, so far as is known, no scientist has reported finding a girl or anyone else living inside one of these atoms.

During the 1980s, researchers developed several new and highly specialized microscopes. The confocal laser scanning microscrope (CLSM) is technically a light microscope; it has an objective lens and uses a very narrowly focused laser light source. The light passes through both the lens and the specimen, then is reflected back through the lens and into a light detector. The detector transforms the reflected light into an electrical signal that can be recorded by a computer, which

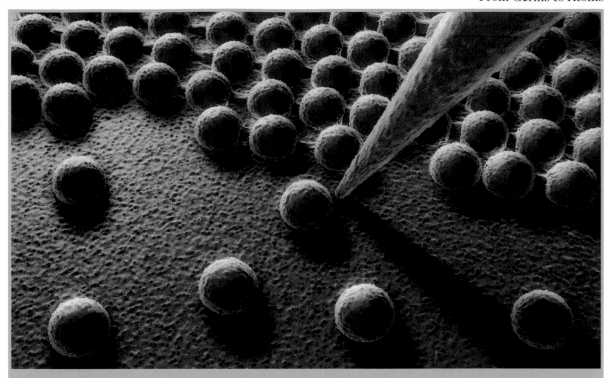

USING THE EXTREMELY FINE PROBE OF AN ATOMIC FORCE MICROSCOPE, TECHNICIANS CAN MOVE ATOMS BY MANIPULATING THE WEAK ELECTRICAL FORCE THAT OCCURS NATURALLY BETWEEN THE ATOMS AND THE PROBE.

then creates an image from the signal. The CLSM produces high-resolution three-dimensional images and can be used on fairly thick specimens. Another instrument, the scanning tunneling microscope (STM), moves a probe with an extremely tiny tip across a specimen's surface, recording naturally occurring variations in the electrical force between the probe and the individual atoms of the surface. When used in a vacuum, the STM can generate enough current to manipulate and rearrange atoms like building blocks. Researchers in the science of materials have used STMs to spell out words by moving atoms. They have even created nano-scale machines, such as a usable abacus with atoms in place of counting beads. Another tool for imaging and manipulating atoms is the atomic force microscope (AFM), invented in 1986. It also uses a probe with an extremely fine tip that reacts to natural variations in electrical force at the atomic level. In their different ways, all of these machines are helping scientists continue the adventure that microscopists like Hooke and Leeuwenhoek began centuries ago: the exploration of the invisible world.

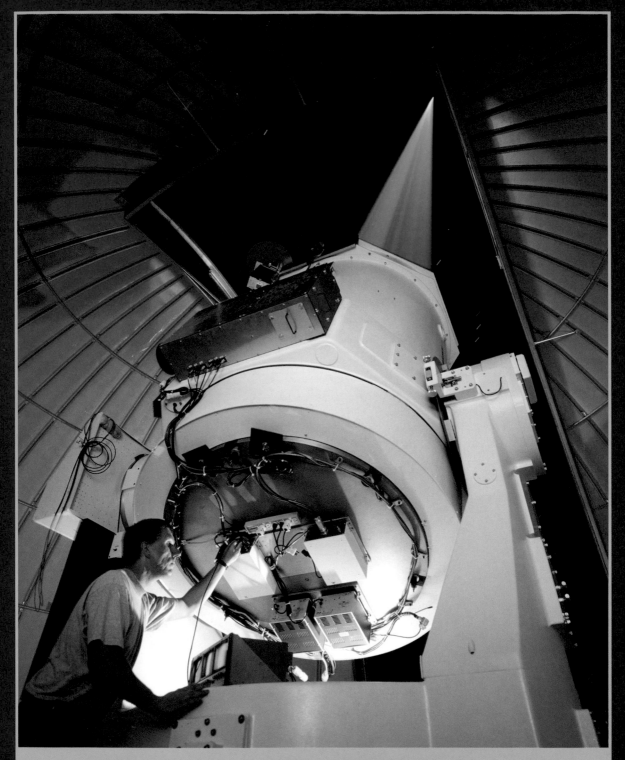

A GREEN LASER BEAM SHOOTS SKYWARD FROM A TELESCOPE AT THE STARFIRE OPTICAL RANGE IN NEW MEXICO, CREATING AN ARTIFICAL "STAR" IN THE HIGH ATMOSPHERE. A LARGER TELESCOPE NEARBY HAS THE LASER STAR IN ITS FIELD OF VISION. AN ADAPTIVE OPTICS PROGRAM ATTACHED TO THE LARGER SCOPE DETECTS CHANGES IN THE LASER STAR'S APPEARANCE CAUSED BY AIR TURBULENCE AND AUTOMATICALLY ADJUSTS THE INSTRUMENT'S MIRROR TO COMPENSATE FOR THEM. THIS ELIMINATES MUCH OF THE "TWINKLE" THAT INTERFERES WITH OBSERVATION OF THE STARS.

# SEVEN

# Many Uses, New Frontiers

Telescopes and microscopes have become part of everyday life in a multitude of ways. The instruments that once amazed Galileo are now toys for some. Anyone can buy an inexpensive telescope and see craters on the Moon or the rings of Saturn. A child's first science kit is likely to contain a microscope better than Robert Hooke's. Still, despite being familiar and accessible to almost everyone, the telescope and the microscope have not lost their power to astonish.

People have many uses for telescopes in various forms: binoculars, sighting scopes on guns, spotting scopes used by bird-watchers and photographers. By far the biggest use of telescopes, however, is in astrophysics—and not always at professional observatories. There are thousands of amateur astronomers around the world. Some buy telescopes; others make their own. Many telescope makers model their creations on the work of John Dobson, a co-founder of the Sidewalk Astronomy movement, who has taught people how to make fairly large, high-quality telescopes easily and affordably. And although some amateur astronomers simply enjoy the occasional night of stargazing, perhaps picking out a few double stars or locating famous celestial landmarks such as the Horsehead Nebula, others are deeply involved in current trends in astrophysics. They communicate with other amateurs and with professional astronomers. They take astronomical photographs and post them on the Internet. They hold star parties, gatherings in locations with good viewing conditions, where as many as several thousand people may point their telescopes at the sky to observe the close approach of Mars, or a meteor shower, or a supernova.

Amateur astonomers also make significant discoveries. In 1995 an Arizona amateur named Tom Bopp, using a homemade telescope, discovered a new comet at the same time a professional astronomer named Alan Hale spotted it. Named Hale-Bopp, the newly discovered celestial wanderer made a spectacular appearance over the following two years, becoming the most photographed comet in history. Four years later, during a meteor shower, two American amateurs were among the first observers to witness confirmed meteor strikes on the Moon. An Australian amateur has discovered more than three dozen supernovas, and in 2003 a South African amateur, a member of a worldwide group called the Center for Backyard Astrophysics, responded to an e-mail alert from the American Association of Variable Star Observers about a gamma-ray burst—a powerful explosion in deep space—and located the source of the burst before a professional did. Astronomy and astrophysics are the only sciences in which professionals and amateurs cooperate and communicate so freely, and in which amateurs make many important discoveries and contributions.

Microscopy, too, has thousands of amateur practitioners. Important discoveries by amateur microscopists are rare these days because, although the sky and the homemade telescope are readily available to almost anyone, the specimens and equipment needed for advanced microscopic research are usually available only to universities, corporations, and other institutions. But a dedicated amateur can explore the microscopic world in a level of detail that would have been impossible to professionals just a couple of generations ago. One of the most active and impressive areas of amateur microscopy is photomicroscopy. Camera and microscope companies regularly sponsor contests for the best images taken by amateurs through microscopes.

On the professional level, microscopes have uses in dozens of fields. Medical technicians use them to analyze samples from patients. Microscopes hang over operating tables so that surgeons can look through them while performing microsurgery, such as stitching together a severed capillary; some surgical microscopes have multiple eyepieces so that several members of an operating-room team can use them at once. Engineers use microscopes to test materials for flaws; archaeologists use them to study pollen from ancient sites in order to learn what plants the inhabitants grew; geologists use them to identify the fossils of minute water creatures so that they can map the boundaries of ancient seas. Microscopes have many uses in law enforcement, too, from analyzing evidence such as paint chips and carpet fibers to comparing tiny marks on bullets that may link a particular gun to a crime.

TWO SURGEONS SHARE A DUAL-HEAD SURGICAL MICROSCOPE WHILE OPERATING ON A PATIENT. USING MICROSCOPES, DOCTORS CAN OPERATE ON MINUTE STRUCTURES SUCH AS CAPILLARIES AND NERVES.

One of the next frontiers of microscope technology will be achieving smaller resolution—perhaps even seeing things smaller than atoms. In 2000 researchers at the University of Augsburg in Germany announced that they had made the first microscopic observations of subatomic particles in action. Using an advanced new type of atomic force microscope, they had captured images of the wing-shaped paths of electrons orbiting an atomic nucleus. The announcement aroused controversy, but three years later a University of Utah team revealed the results of a mathematical study that demonstrated that microscopic imaging of electron orbits was possible. Although most physicists believe it is impossible to view subatomic particles directly, future research in atomic force microscopy may yield further images of their movements. Electron microscopes, too, are being extended to subatomic levels. In 2004 the U.S. Department of Energy funded a project in which an Oregon manufacturer of electron microscopes is building a new scanning and transmission electron microscope (STEM) that will achieve a resolution of 0.5 angstrom, about one-third the size of a carbon atom.

The manufacture of very small components such as semiconductors and computer chips led the way to nanotechnology, the development of microscopic tools. This pioneering field is young but promising. One of the most exciting recent advances in nanotechnology concerns a microscopic microscope. In 2002 bioengineer Luke P. Lee of the University of California at Berkeley announced the invention of a microlens, a bubble of polymer smaller than the period at the end of this sentence, attached to an extremely small scanner. The device was used to make an image of a plant cell. That image proved identical to an image made of the same specimen with a confocal laser scanning microscope, demonstrating that the microlens works. Lee called the device "a microscope that is five hundred to one thousand times smaller than anything in its class." If successfully developed for use, the microlens could be part of a small, portable medical testing device that Lee calls "lab-on-a-chip." It could even be inserted into a patient to let doctors watch cancer cells respond to medication.

ASTRONOMERS CONSIDER THE 165-INCH (4.2-METER) HERSCHEL TELESCOPE ON LA PALMA, AN ISLAND IN THE CANARY GROUP IN THE ATLANTIC OCEAN, ONE OF THE BEST REFLECTORS IN THE WORLD. ITS NAME HONORS WILLIAM HERSCHEL, WHO BUILT TELESCOPES AND, AMONG OTHER THINGS, DISCOVERED THE PLANET URANUS. THE INSTRUMENT IS PART OF THE ISAAC NEWTON GROUP OF TELESCOPES, NAMED FOR THE SCIENTIST WHOSE RESEARCHES INTO OPTICS CAN STAND AS A SYMBOL OF OUR ONGOING QUEST FOR BETTER INSIGHT INTO THE COSMOS AND THE WORLD AROUND US.

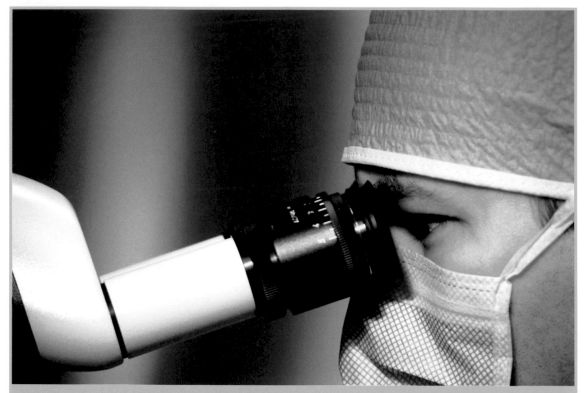

THE MICROSCOPE, IN ALL ITS VARIOUS FORMS, HAS OPENED UP A ONCE INACCESSIBLE—AND UNSEEABLE—WORLD.

As for telescopes, astrophysicists and engineers have given much thought to the future of far-seeing devices. Some of their proposals are for larger, more powerful versions of telescopes that already exist. Other ideas are visions of entirely new kinds of instruments. Scores of ground-based and space-based optical, radio, UV, and IR instruments are now under construction or being planned. Speculations about longer-term possibilities have included an observatory on the far side of the Moon, where the sky is permanently dark; optical telescopes with liquid mirrors consisting of giant rotating dishes of mercury; and an OWL—a 3,937-inch, 100-meter Overwhelmingly Large Telescope—in space. Some or none of these visions may become reality, but one thing is certain: Leeuwenhoek's "craving after knowledge" is shared by many people. Those who use microscopes and telescopes to explore the realms of the very small and the very vast will keep searching for ways to extend their vision into the unknown.

# Glossary

**angstrom**—A unit of measurement equal to one ten-billionth of a meter.

**aperture**—The opening in a telescope through which light enters the instrument.

**astrophysics**—The study of all physical properties of heavenly bodies, including chemical composition, density, luminousness, and mass.

**binocular**—An instrument for use with both eyes that makes distant objects appear closer.

**chromatic aberration**—The illusion of a rainbow-like blur or fringe that can surround an image viewed through a lens.

**compound microscope**—A microscope that uses more than one lens, multiplying its magnifying power.

**cosmology**—Scientific or philosophic theory about the origin and structure of the universe.

**electron microscope**—A microscope that uses a focused beam of electrons to examine an object; can be used to view objects too small to be seen through an optical microscope.

**lens**—A disc-shaped piece of transparent material with one or both sides curved outward (convex) or inward (concave); used to bend and focus light rays.

**light microscope**—Another name for an optical microscope.

**magnifying glass**—A handheld lens used to make things appear larger.

**micrometer**—A unit of measurement equal to one-millionth of a meter; sometimes called a micron.

**microscope**—A viewing instrument that makes small, close objects appear larger; used to view things not visible to unaided eyesight; see simple microscope and compound microscope.

**microscopy**—The art and science of using microscopes.

**nanometer**—A unit of measurement equal to one-billionth of a meter.

**optical**—Having to do with light and vision; relating to optics.

**optical microscope**—A microscope that uses light to illuminate the object being examined and uses a lens or multiple lenses to magnify it.

**optics**—The science of light and its behavior; includes the optical properties of materials and the physics of vision; optics in a telescope or microscope are its lenses and mirrors.

**radio telescope**—A combination of antenna and radio receiver used to gather radio waves from the sky.

**reflector**—A telescope in which light rays are focused by a mirror or mirrors.

**refractor**—A telescope in which light rays are focused by a lens or lenses.

**simple microscope**—A microscope that uses only one lens; basically a magnifying glass in a tube or frame.

**spectroscope**—An instrument that splits light into a set of wavelengths that identify the elements of which the light source is made; an image made with a spectroscope is called a spectrograph.

**telescope**—A viewing instrument that makes distant objects appear closer.

**telescopy**—The art and science of using telescopes.

1300s
Europeans use lenses to improve or correct vision.

1543
Nicolaus Copernicus publishes a description of the solar system in which the Earth and other planets revolve around the Sun.

about 1590
Dutch spectacle makers may have invented the first compound microscope by combining two lenses.

1608
Hans Lippershey of the Netherlands tries to patent a refracting telescope to be used as a spyglass.

1609
Galileo Galilei makes astronomical observations through a telescope; that year or in 1610 he also constructs a compound microscope he calls an *occhialino*.

1665
Robert Hooke publishes *Micrographia*, describing the first biological studies made using the microscope.

**1674**

Antoni van Leeuwenhoek improves the simple microscope for use in biological study.

**1668**

Isaac Newton makes the first reflector, a telescope using a mirror.

**1770s–1780s**

William Herschel builds telescopes; he discovers the planet Uranus in 1781.

**1830**

Joseph Jackson Lister improves the objective lens arrangement of the compound microscope.

**1840**

American Henry Draper makes the first known astronomical photograph, a picture of the Moon.

**1845**

In Ireland, William Parsons builds a reflector with a 72-inch (1.8-meter) mirror.

**1872**

Ernst Abbe develops a mathematical formula that allows for maximum resolution in microscopes.

**1917**

The 100-inch (2.5-meter) Hooker Telescope is completed at Mount Wilson Observatory, California.

**1931**
Ernst Ruska and Max Knoll build the first electron microscope.

**1932**
Frits Zernike invents the phase contrast microscope.

**1948**
The 200-inch (5-meter) Hale Telescope is completed at Palomar Mountain Observatory, California.

**1951**
Erwin Müller becomes the first to see individual atoms using a microscope.

**1955**
Jodrell Bank Observatory, England, is site of world's first large, steerable radio telescope.

**1967**
Müller combines spectroscopy and the field ion microscope, making it possible to chemically identify individual atoms.

**1975**
The first astronomical observation using a charge-coupled device (CCD) is made.

**1980s**
The scanning tunneling microscope and atomic force microscope are introduced.

1990

The United States launches the Hubble Space Telescope, the first orbiting telescope.

1993, 1996

The Keck I and Keck II telescopes begin operation at Mauna Kea, Hawaii.

1998

The Very Large Telescope (VLT) begins operation at Paranal Observatory in Chile.

2000

German researchers announce the microscopic imaging of orbiting electrons.

2003

NASA launches the Spitzer Space Telescope, the fourth and last in its Great Observatories series of space telescopes.

2005

The Southern African Large Telescope (SALT) begins operation.

These are some useful Web sites about microscopes and telescopes. Information is available at many other sites as well. Since this book was written, these sites may have changed, moved to new addresses, or gone out of existence. New sites may now be available.

Optics for Kids
www.opticsforkids.org
Interactive tutorial in the basic principles of optics, with information on how lenses and mirrors are used in microscopes and telescopes.

Microscopes
www.nobelprize.org/physics/educational/micrroscopes/index.html
Maintained by the Nobel Foundation, which awards the world's most respected prizes in science and other fields, this educational site gives an overview of milestones in microscopy and offers interactive simulators for four types of modern microscopes.

History of Microscopes

http://inventors.about.com/od/mstartinventions/a/microscopes.htm

A timeline for the development of microscopes from their origins in spectacle-making to the inventions of the 1980s.

Optics and Microscopy

www.micro.magnet.fsu.edu

Florida State University maintains Molecular Expressions, a site devoted to optics and microscopy, with dozens of links to sites with how-to and historical information; includes interactive tutorials on refraction and reflection, as well as galleries of photographs taken through microscopes.

Virtual Library: Microscopy

www.ou.edu/research/electron/www-vl/

Sponsored by the Samuel Roberts Electron Microscopy Laboratory and the University of Oklahoma, this site links to information on all types of microscopes, microscopy in fields such as biology and medicine, and numerous other microsope-related sites.

Telescopes from the Ground Up

http://amazing-space.stsci.edu/resources/explorations/groundup

Part of Amazing Space, a web site for students and teachers maintained by the Space Telescope Science Institute, this site explores the history of telescopes from Galileo to NASA.

All about Hubble

www.pbs.org/deepspace/hubble/index.html

The Space Telescope Science Institute developed this page for the PBS Mysteries of Deep Space web site. It includes information about the Hubble's equipment and its mission, as well as a link to a NASA site that tracks the Hubble in real time.

Virtual Tour of an Observatory
http://mcdonaldobservatory.org/visitors/tour/
Photos and a virtual video tour of the University of Texas's McDonald Observatory, the home of several large scopes and the site of a leading astronomy research and education program.

American Association of Amateur Astronomers
www.astromax.org
This site offers amateur astronomers, or anyone interested in learning more about amateur astronomers and their scientific contributions, information about telescopes, the solar system, the universe, and astronomy clubs and publications.

Sidewalk Astronomers
www.sidewalkastronomers.com
Background on John Dobson, co-founder of the Sidewalk Astronomers, and on the principles and practices of this grass-roots movement in amateur astronomy, with links to sites offering information on building a Dobsonian telescope.

# Bibliography

FOR STUDENTS

Asimov, Isaac. *Eyes on the Universe: A History of the Telescope.* Boston: Houghton Mifflin, 1975.

Ford, Brian J. *Single Lens: The Story of the Simple Microscope.* New York: Harper & Row, 1985.

Gallant, Roy A. *Earth's Place in Space.* New York: Benchmark Books, 2000.

Kerrod, Robin. *Hubble: The Mirror on the Universe.* Buffalo, NY: Firefly Books, 2003.

MacLachlan, James. *Galileo Galilei: First Physicist.* New York: Oxford University Press, 1997.

Rogers, Kirsteen. *The Usborne Complete Book of the Microscope.* London: Usborne House, 1998.

Spangenburg, Ray and Kit Moser. *The Hubble Space Telescope*. New York: Franklin Watts, 2002.

Stewart, Gail B. *Microscopes: Bringing the Unseen World into Focus.* San Diego, CA: Lucent Books, 1992.

Voit, Mark. *Hubble Space Telescope: New Views of the Universe.* New York: Harry N. Abrams, Inc. and the Smithsonian Institution, 2000.

FOR TEACHERS OR ADVANCED READERS

Bourely, France. *Hidden Beauty: Microworlds Revealed.* New York: Harry N. Abrams, Inc., 2002.

Burke, Bernard F. and Francis Graham-Smith. *An Introduction to Radio Astronomy.* 2nd edition. New York: Cambridge University Press, 2002.

Florence, Ronald. *The Perfect Machine: Building the Palomar Telescope.* New York: HarperCollins, 1994.

Gest, Howard. *Microbes: An Invisible Universe.* Washington, DC: ASM Press, 2003.

King, Henry C. *The History of the Telescope.* Mineola, NY: Dover Publications, 2003. Originally published 1955.

Panek, Richard. *Seeing and Believing: The Story of the Telescope, or How We Found Our Place in the Universe.* London: Fourth Estate, 2000.

Pendergrast, Mark. *Mirror Mirror: A History of the Human Love Affair with Reflection.* New York: Basic Books, 2004.

Ruestow, Edward Grant. *The Microscope in the Dutch Republic: The Shaping of Discovery.* Cambridge, UK: Cambridge University Press, 1996.

Watson, Fred. *Stargazer: The Life and Times of the Telescope.* Cambridge, MA: Da Capo Press, 2005.

Zirker, J. B. *An Acre of Glass: A History and Forecast of the Telescope.* Baltimore: Johns Hopkins University Press, 2005.

# Index

Page numbers for illustrations are in **boldface**.

# About the Author

Rebecca Stefoff has written numerous nonfiction books for readers of all ages. In addition to books about science, nature, and exploration, her works include biographies of historical and literary figures. Stefoff wrote *The Telephones* and *Submarines* for the Benchmark Books Great Inventions series, and she has written about discoveries and their effects in other works, such as *Charles Darwin and the Evolution Revolution* (Oxford University Press, 1996). Stefoff is the author of the ten-volume Benchmark Books series North American Historial Atlases and the five-volume World Historical Atlases series. You can find more information about her books for young readers at www.rebeccastefoff.com